THE
WAY
TO
BEA

THE
WAY
TO
BEA

KAT YEH

LITTLE, BROWN AND COMPANY
New York Boston

Text copyright © 2017 by Kat Yeh
Illustrations copyright © 2017 by Aimee Sicuro

Cover art copyright © 2017 by Aimee Sicuro. Cover design by Marcie Lawrence. Cover copyright © 2017 by Hachette Book Group, Inc.

Little, Brown and Company

Hachette Book Group
1290 Avenue of the Americas, New York, NY 10104
Visit us at lb-kids.com

First Edition: September 2017

Little, Brown and Company is a division of Hachette Book Group, Inc.
The Little, Brown name and logo are trademarks of Hachette Book Group, Inc.

The publisher is not responsible for websites (or their content) that are not owned by the publisher.

Library of Congress Cataloging-in-Publication Data
Names: Yeh, Kat, author.
Title: The way to Bea / by Kat Yeh.
Description: First edition. | New York : Little, Brown and Company, 2017. |
Summary: Recently estranged from her best friend and weeks away from shifting from only child to big sister, seventh grader Beatrix Lee consoles herself by writing haiku in invisible ink and hiding the poems, but one day she finds a reply—is it the librarian with all the answers, the editor of the school paper who admits to admiring her poetry, an old friend feeling remorse, or the boy obsessed with visiting the local labyrinth?
Identifiers: LCCN 2016051845 | ISBN 9780316236676 (hardcover) |
ISBN 9780316236652 (ebook) | ISBN 9780316236720 (library edition ebook)
Subjects: | CYAC: Poetry—Fiction. | Authorship—Fiction. | Newspapers—Fiction. | Labyrinths—Fiction. | Best friends—Fiction. | Friendship—Fiction. | Family life—Fiction. | Middle schools—Fiction. | Schools—Fiction. | Taiwanese Americans—Fiction.
Classification: LCC PZ7.Y3658 Way 2017 | DDC [Fic]—dc23
LC record available at https://lccn.loc.gov/2016051845

ISBNs: 978-0-316-23667-6 (hardcover), 978-0-316-23665-2 (ebook)

Printed in the United States of America

LSC-C

10 9 8 7 6 5 4 3 2 1

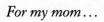

For my mom . . .

When I'm figuring out a haiku, I place my right hand on my chest like we do at school for the Pledge of Allegiance. The first line of a haiku is always five syllables, and I like to count out each beat, starting with my pinky finger and working my way across.

one, two, three, four, five

I know it's exactly right when my thumb gives that final thump *(five)* over my heart.

There are only three lines in a haiku.

The first has five beats
the second has seven beats
and the last has five.

(Five, seven, five)

Haiku are nothing like the poems I used to write. Those were free verse, which is exactly what it sounds like. Poems that are loose and flowy and free. The kind you sing or shout or paint all over your bedroom walls. With free verse, you can pretty much do whatever you want.

A haiku is different. One wrong choice and you have to go back and start again.

But it doesn't even matter how different they are, because all poems begin the same way: from something you feel inside. Like being mesmerized by the sound of certain words. Or feeling sad that you're alone at the turn of a path.

Or being afraid.

A poem could begin one night when you're so lost and afraid that the last thing you're even thinking about is writing one. But the words will come anyway, whether you want them to or not, and you will find yourself with your hand on your chest, just like the Pledge of Allegiance, counting out the beats.

I do not know the way

Until that extra thump *(six)* on your heart tells you that you've made the wrong choice. Only this time, it's not just a haiku—it's real life. And there's no starting over.

Chapter 1

There are things that are okay to say out loud and things that should definitely just stay in your head. Everyone knows that.

Except maybe Mr. Clarke.

The official name of his class is Social Studies: Ancient Civilizations, but he always likes to say the colon along with the rest of it.

As in, "Good morning and welcome to Social Studies *Colon* Ancient Civilizations!"

He says it every day like it's the funniest thing ever.

Like he doesn't know how weird this is. Mr. Clarke doesn't know a lot of things. I mean, he knows social studies, but he doesn't know that it's too much to come back from summer with a full beard that he's slowly trimming away and changing each week. We've been in school for a month now, and so far, he's had a caveman, a Viking braid, a waxed beard with a pointy tip, and now, muttonchops.

Today, I'm late as usual. I try to open the door as quietly as possible so I can just slip in, but the second my head appears, Mr. Clarke calls out, "Welcome, welcome, Miss Beatrix *Harper?* Lee!"

Mr. Clarke's been trying to guess my middle name since the beginning of the year. I know he just wants to be funny, but does he always have to make such a scene? This is my only class with S, and all I want is to get through it with as little attention as possible. I don't want to talk, I don't want to be called on, and I definitely don't want to be part of any scenes.

But so far, every day in this class feels like that game— the one where everyone takes turns pulling the blocks out of a tower, then when it topples over, they all yell *Jenga!* No matter how hard you try, the tower always falls.

"Hurry, hurry, now, Beatrix!"

I put my head down and quickly make my way in, pulling my headphones onto my neck. I reach for my phone to check my splitter. I got it this summer in Taiwan. Most splitters are just boring, but this one is shaped like a smiley bunny face that clicks into the headphone jack. You can connect two sets of headphones into the two bunny ears whenever you want to listen to the same song with someone else. I just haven't had a chance to use it yet.

The whole class is standing around a large table up front. I find a spot across from where S is huddled with L and L and A.

Out of the corner of my eye, I see a swish of pale hair and think maybe S is looking at me, but when I turn to check, I hear "Ow!" and realize I've clonked the boy next to me, because I still have my backpack on. What's his name? Justin something? I turn the other way to try and slip it off, but then—"Hey!"—I whack into Kirsten Henry on the other side. She shoots me an annoyed look. I don't even really know Kirsten. She's from one of the two other elementary schools that come together in our middle school.

People start craning their necks to see what's going on. I grip the straps of my backpack tightly and stare straight ahead. I just won't move again for the next hour. If Kirsten and Justin want an apology, they'll be waiting a long time. I haven't said a single word in this class yet, and I'm not going to start now. I try to focus on whatever it is on the table in front of us.

It's a big wooden maze.

Mr. Clarke is standing behind it with Dan Ross.

He clears his throat. "For his presentation today, Dan has chosen the topic 'Politics in Ancient Greece.' I will thank you in advance for being courteous and giving him your full attention."

Dan smirks. "Long ago in ancient Greece, King Minos, son of the almighty Zeus, commanded that a labyrinth be built to house his man-eating beast, the Minotaur."

Mr. Clarke drums his fingers on his chin in the space between his muttonchops. "Fascinating start, Dan. Are you sure this isn't a report on Greek mythology?"

"Nah," says Dan. "It's ancient Greek politics. It's political because there's a king."

"Fair enough." Mr. Clarke nods. "And while we're

8

at it, class, how about an Extra Credit Curveball! Draw a map of Zeus's family tree. Hint: you'll need big paper and a strong stomach. Please continue, Dan. I can't wait to see where this goes."

"The labyrinth of King Minos was an impossible maze where he'd throw all his prisoners. I got this one from my cousin. My mom gave it to him for his birthday, but he didn't like it." Dan shrugs. "He's kinda weird. Anyway, today my weird cousin's maze will demonstrate what happens to those who wander in the Labyrinth of Minos!"

I feel sorry for this cousin who has to go through life being related to Dan Ross. Dan has been a sworn enemy since his birthday party in kindergarten, when he told me his dog was one of the Killer Hounds of Leland Estate that got kicked out for being too ferocious. I cried and cried because I've always been afraid of big dogs, but S held him around the neck, petting him. She said as long as I acted like I wasn't afraid, he wouldn't hurt me. But how does someone do that? Act like something they're not? We swore never to speak to Dan again.

S's voice rings clearly across the room. "Whooo-hoo! Dan the Man!"

Then A chimes in, "Yeah, Dan!"

Mr. Clarke rises up on his tiptoes and carefully studies the maze from above. "Unnecessary comment about your cousin aside, I will say that this is a very impressive maze, and it looks like . . . yes, it is. It's a perfect maze."

"Thank you! Thank you!" Dan bows and waves. "No applause, just throw money."

Mr. Clarke pats him on the back. "*Perfect* refers to the specific type of maze you have here. A perfect maze is actually one of the only mazes that can be solved quite easily. Which I believe merits another Extra Credit Curveball if anyone can tell me how."

I stand on my tiptoes and look down at the maze the way Mr. Clarke did. I like how all the walls are connected together. Connected and holding each other up. With no lonely wall left stranded by itself.

A perfect maze.

It sounds like something that should be in a poem.

When I close my eyes, I can see things more clearly. I can imagine how I would write and draw a poem about a perfect maze. The words could wind around the page, maybe filled with curling vines that climb along a turning path, up and around and...

"Why, yes, Beatrix!"

With a start, I open my eyes to giggling in the room. My hand is raised, my finger tracing words in the air. I feel my cheeks go hot and shake my head no as I shove my hands deep into my pockets, where I plan to keep them for the rest of the year.

Dan Ross snorts. "It doesn't matter how easy it is to solve, Mr. Clarke," he says. "Hammy'll never make it." That's when I see he's holding a little ball of fur. "She's too scared. Watch—*boo!*" She squirms in his grip and he laughs. "Wait'll you see what happens when she gets stuck in a dead end."

"First of all, Dan, the proper term for a dead end in a maze is a blind alley. And I say give little Hammy here a chance. She's got it in her, maybe she just doesn't know it yet." Mr. Clarke reaches over and scratches Hammy on the head.

"You're just saying that because you haven't met the Minotaur yet!" Dan pulls out an action figure with rows

11

of teeth and a long, whippy tail. "The Ridley Scott Alien, circa 1979." He turns to Mr. Clarke. "My dad keeps it up on a shelf in the original sealed box."

Mr. Clarke frowns. "Uh, perhaps that had better go back in the box."

Dan shrugs. "Can't have a maze without a monster in the middle."

And he drops Hammy in, headfirst.

I push forward as Hammy tumbles down in an awkward somersault and scrambles to her feet, her teeny little hamster sides panting. I can almost hear her heart pitter-pattering away. She doesn't even move at first. She doesn't know which way to go. It's not fair.

Hammy looks *left* to the path that leads to the exit and then *right* to the path that leads to the blind alley. Left...right...left...

Right!

She makes a bobbling run straight into the dead end.

Hammy hits the wall and turns in a circle. Stops and then turns again. She pants for a second and then starts clawing at the dead end, trying to get through.

Dan snickers. "Now watch what happens...." And he starts to sneak the alien right behind her.

"Dan..." Mr. Clarke warns.

I look at Mr. Clarke. Then at Hammy in the maze. I can't even imagine how scared she is, trapped and trying to get out—and that Dan Ross! He's still the same. Scaring people—and hamsters!—just because he can. Why won't someone stop him? Why won't anyone stand up to his stupid, smirking—

Dan laughs as he raises the alien up—

And someone screams out, *"NO!"*

Wait.

Who was—

I clap a hand over my mouth.

My eyes dart over to where A and L and L are cracking up. And S is just staring at the floor. Worried someone will remember that up till a month ago, we were best friends.

Jenga.

I turn and run out.

Chapter 2

I rush down the hall and push through the exit, running across the soccer field, into the woods, and onto the path that leads home. I don't stop until I get to the clearing by the Wall.

It's like stepping into a safe zone. I let myself collapse onto the ground and try to catch my breath.

No one knows who made the paths that wind through the little woods and feed into all the streets in our neighborhood. They've just always been there. Maybe since the very first houses here on Long Island were built. They connect our street to S and L and L's streets and then to the main path, where you can take a left to the elementary school, a right to the middle school, or an even farther right to, well, to pretty much anywhere. Over the years, we've searched every inch of every path, and ours is the only one with a stone wall.

We were little the first time we came upon our crumbling Wall, and it looked like a stone creature to us, hunched over like a baby elephant in the clearing. We ran back to my parents' studio, yelling, "Why is there a wall in the woods? What is it? Where did it come from?"

Without looking up, Dad yelled, "Portal to the land of the goblin king!" and kept on drawing his comics.

And from her side of the studio, Mom called out, "Portal to the underworld!" and threw more black paint on her canvas.

Just as quickly as we'd come in, we ran back out to check the Wall for clues.

It might have been left over from an old mansion. Or a prison gate. Or a secret tower. But it didn't matter; it was ours. And the best part was that it had this... opening. Nothing special to look at. Just the kind of small dark hole you'd expect to find filled with crawling beetles and maybe moss. But it was more than that. Because when we pressed our eyes to it, we could see that it reached farther and deeper than any ordinary crawling-beetle-and-maybe-moss-filled hole should. As if the inside were bigger than the outside.

We named it the Portal.

We whispered our deepest secrets into it. We asked it our scariest questions. We could tell it anything. Inside the Portal was the safest place we knew.

A twig snaps.

I force myself not to look up. Because when you're waiting for someone on a path, every twig will snap and every bush will rustle, but no one will ever be there. No one ever is. Not in the mornings when I wait here until I'm late for school every day and not now.

And there's no way S would run after me after the scene I made.

Barging in late and crashing into everyone with my backpack.

Doing my weird skywriting in front of the whole class.

Ugh. And then screaming *NO!* like I was at a horror movie and not just watching a class presentation.

Why?

Why, why, WHY do I always have to be so...

...me.

For the first time, I'm glad I still have my backpack on. I squirm out of it and unzip the front section, scrabbling around until my fingers touch what I'm looking for. I close my eyes and take a deep breath.

People do different things to calm down or relax. My mom starts a painting. My dad shops online for new inks and old pens.

I make poems.

My hand finds the stack of paper I cut into little three-by-three-inch squares and I can already feel my breathing slow. Next is a small glass bottle.

Lemon juice with exactly three drops of water in it. Invisible ink.

We learned all about invisible ink from this book called *Start Your Own Secret Club* that S and L and L and I got from the book club flyer at school when we were in third grade. There are lots of different formulas, but the best is lemon juice and water. To make the ink visible, you need someone to light a match and carefully hold it underneath.

The book has all these funny cartoons with this guy who explains what to do. My favorite one is where he's peeking from behind a tree, watching this girl read his invisible letter. His voice bubble says *Now all you have to do is wait for your friend to light a match, and your message will be received!* But it takes her so long to get the matches to light that by the time she finally does, he has this long white beard and he's all mad and she sees that the message says *Can you bring me a sandwich? I'm hungry!*

In the book, it says you can use a cotton swab to dip and write your message, but that just doesn't feel very poetic to me. I use this dip pen I stole from my dad. It has a golden nib etched with curly lines and tipped with a fat sort of nubbin. I wonder if he's even noticed that it's missing. He's been pretty busy, so he isn't really noticing much lately.

I want to write something, but I'm not sure what and that makes me think of this thing my mom always says: *Whatever you feel on the inside is what you put out there in the universe.*

And what I'm thinking about now is Hammy and the maze and how unfair it is when you think a path will lead you somewhere amazing and you just end up running into a dead end.

I close my eyes, hold my hand over my heart, and count out the beats of words that come from the inside.

     if you are in a maze ... (six).

Start again.

     a blind alley up ahead ... (seven).

No.

     tell me why, my friend (five)
     blind allies have to appear (seven)
     on the paths we walk (five)

Five, seven, five.

Thumb over my heart on the last beat.

Haiku.

The way I know when something I've written is perfect is that I feel truly connected to it in a way I didn't before. It's like the words and the feeling behind the words are coming right from my heart. Whether they're happy or wondering or sad, they just feel right and real and right.

I dip my pen into the invisible ink and write the words down. They shine bright and clear, made up of lemony water and whatever it is inside me that makes poems want to be in the world. I quickly close my eyes again before they can evaporate.

I know the whole point of invisible ink is to make things disappear, but today, this thought makes a little sting in my heart. Because no matter how long I wait out here, no matter how many snapping twigs or rustling bushes I hear, I know that no one is coming with a light to make my words visible again. And after all the thinking and feeling and writing, all I'm really left with is an invisible haiku that doesn't belong anywhere.

I open my eyes and see the Portal.

I stare for a second—then begin to roll the little paper as tight and tiny as I can. I search the ground and pull up a long piece of grass. The kind that's sturdy and wide. The kind you can make a long, loud whistle from when you hold it between your thumbs and blow. I wrap the grass around the roll twice and tie it.

I hear nearby rustling and quickly look side to side, but I'm still alone.

I take a deep breath.

Look into the Portal.

And tuck my invisible haiku inside.

Safe.

I'm about to walk away, but then I stop and grab the pack of matches I keep in my backpack for testing out my invisible inks. And I tuck that in, too.

Because even invisible things deserve to have a little hope.

Chapter 3

The one time S and I tried to sneak out of study hall in sixth grade, we got caught, and she said it was all my fault because I had come up with this elaborate plan and then panicked and couldn't stop laughing. *Bea, your problem is you're just—you're too much. Just act like it's no big deal. Walk fast, but not too fast. If you walk too fast, they'll know something's up. It's all about Going Stealth.* Of course I believed her. She knew all about this kind of stuff from her brother, Jay, who's a year older.

So who would have guessed I'd be the one sneaking

off campus every single day since seventh grade began? Though the truth is that I don't usually cut classes. Just lunch. I sneak out here to the Wall every day, so I don't have to face the cafeteria. Being out here during an actual class feels strange, and I want to head back in. Also, I just really don't want any of my teachers to be mad at me.

I peek out from behind a tree.

I may have bolted across the middle of the soccer field on the way out. But there's only one way to make it back in. Go Stealth. I sneak around the soccer field, staying hidden in the trees, and slip back into the building with no problem. First period has just ended. It's noisy and crowded in the halls. All I have to do is blend in. Try to be as anonymous as possible. I let out a sigh of relief.

I'll talk to Mr. Clarke tomorrow and just tell him I had to go to the bathroom. How could anyone get in trouble for going to the bathroom? I'll say I had a stomach-ache or something and then decided to go straight to second-period study hall. Who would question that?

And then I suddenly remember something about second-period study hall. I yank out my phone and look at the date. Tuesday. Today is Tuesday. And on Tuesdays, second-period study hall is replaced with—

"Beatrix?"

Oh no.

"Bea?"

Go Stealth. Go Stealth. Go Stealth. I put my head down and walk fast. But it might be too fast, so I slow down. What is Fast But Not Too Fast supposed to feel like anyway?

"Bea!"

Two neon sneakers appear in front of me.

There is no fighting the sneakers.

My favorite librarian, Mrs. Rodriguez, doesn't wear boring grown-up shoes. Mostly because she's not a boring grown-up. If Mrs. Rodriguez were a superhero, her power would be the ability to make every student love her. All the high school kids call her the Rodreeg-inator or Reegster or Reegs. I can't think of any other teachers around here who get nicknames. Today, her sneakers are bright yellow with pink and purple swooshes and they're pointing right at me. I look up.

"Oh...hi, Mrs. Reegs...."

She gives me her I Know You Were Trying to Get Away But I'm Not Going to Call You Out on It Look. She's also slightly out of breath from chasing me down the hall.

"Bea, I hope you didn't forget that on Tuesdays—"

I know what she's going to say, and I have to keep her from saying it. I need to walk in the opposite direction she's going to want me to walk. So I blurt out the first thing that comes to me. "I cut Social Studies Colon Ancient Civilizations!"

It works.

Mrs. Reegs stops short. "*You* cut a class? You cut Mr. Clarke's class? Beatrix!"

I hate for her to think of me this way, but I have more important things at stake. "I'm sorry, but it was Hammy's fault. No, wait—I mean, actually, it was Dan Ross's fault."

"Slow down," Mrs. Reegs says. "Take a breath. Start over. What happened?"

I have to keep her moving away from the other end of the hall. I take a step and she follows me. "Okay, so you know Dan Ross? We ran away from him during recess in second grade, and you had us read the stories about the brother and sister who find the tree house filled with magic books?"

Mrs. Reegs nods.

Another one of her superpowers is that she remembers every single book she's ever given us. She's also the only person at school these days who can get more than two words out of me. By the time I see her, I usually have so many words backed up, they come out like a flood.

"Well, he was doing this presentation for Social Studies Colon Ancient Civilizations that wasn't even political and there was this poor little hamster and his cousin's maze and these dead ends and it was so unfair and I kind of yelled like I was in a horror movie or something and it was so embarrassing that I just ran for it—but I don't want to get detention or suspension or whatever, so can you please, please let me go...over in this direction to explain to Mr. Clarke, so he won't be mad?"

Mrs. Reegs holds up a hand and shuts her eyes. "Okay, Bea. Yes, you need to go and apologize to Mr. Clarke, right now. I'll come with you and it will be fine."

I stop. "Oh. You don't have to come," I say. "I'll be fine. Actually, I feel better already!"

But Mrs. Reegs just points down the hall, and there's no choice but to turn and go.

When we get to Mr. Clarke's classroom, she stays outside the door, because if her superpower is getting along with kids, her kryptonite is making friends with other grown-ups. I don't really get it. Grown-ups are so much easier to talk to than kids.

She gives me a little push.

I step inside and Mr. Clarke looks up from his desk.

As usual, he's all jokes. "Well, it looks like someone's recovered from last period's trauma. Come in, Beatrix! I'll have you know that Hammy survived. I put a stop to her visit with the Minotaur."

He points over to a glass cage lined with newspapers. It has one of those wheels in it and a little food dish. There's a sticker on the glass that says PROPERTY OF MATTIE ROSS DO NOT TUCH (THAT MEENS YOU DAN!) in crooked blue crayon. Hammy is snuggled in a corner behind a little cardboard wall. She looks safe.

27

I'm trying to figure out what to say, but Mr. Clarke just laughs. "Don't look so worried. Just try to come up with a better option than running away next time. All it takes is one person to run, and the next thing you know, someone's chasing after you, and then the whole class, and then who would be left to listen to my charming lectures?"

As if anyone would chase after me.

Mr. Clarke studies my face. "Hmmm. Would you like to help me give Hammy a little snack? I think I have something here." He pulls out a bag of carrot slices and lets me hand one to Hammy. She's so cute, eating it like it's a big orange cookie. "Extra Credit Curveball! If you can name the main health benefits of carrots."

The first day of school, Mr. Clarke told us that his Extra Credit Curveballs were a chance to see that learning with him was about more than just Social Studies Colon Ancient Civilizations. He said they were about the power of information. No matter where it came from or what it was, information could really make a difference in your life. I guess none of us will ever know, because the thing is: no one ever does his Extra Credit Curveballs. You don't even get real points for them. But I don't think he really cares.

"Well, Hammy has now been nourished and rested, so I guess we will see you tomorrow, Miss Beatrix *Potter?* Lee."

I shake my head, but I smile.

"Well then—is that Ms. Rodriguez waiting outside? I'd recognize those sneakers anywhere! Come in, please."

Mrs. Reegs peeks in. "Oh, uh, sorry."

"No need to apologize. You're welcome here anytime. Will you be escorting young Beatrix here to her next class?"

I suddenly remember why I was avoiding Mrs. Reegs and begin to back out of the classroom. But she's too fast. She blocks the doorway with both arms awkwardly. Then looks up at Mr. Clarke. "Oh, sorry—it's just—we're on our way to a *Broadside* meeting. Bea missed the first few meetings, but we're going to make sure she gets to this one! Big day! First-ever seventh-grade poetry editor!" She says this in a way more cheerful voice than it probably needs. She gives Mr. Clarke a thumbs-up. Then she makes this face and stares at her thumb like it went and did that on its own without checking with her first.

Mr. Clarke laughs and says, "Well, you'd better take off, then." And gives her a thumbs-up back. Grown-ups are so strange.

Mrs. Reegs stammers something and then just waves and ushers me out.

Out in the hall, I try to give her a Look that says You Don't Like Talking to Other Grown-Ups, and I Don't Like Talking to Other Kids, So Can't We Call It a Day?

But that doesn't seem to work, so I try:

Something Weird Is Going On with My Best Friend in the World So Maybe Cut Me a Break and Let Me Go?

And finally:

Perhaps You Know My Mom, World-Famous Artist Eve Lee? She Says Whatever You Feel Inside Is What You Put Out in the Universe and I Don't Want to Put Anything Out There Right Now. Especially My Poetry.

But I guess I'm not as good at giving Looks as she is, because Mrs. Reegs has her hand on my shoulder and we're heading the exact opposite way from the way I want to go.

Chapter 4

When Mrs. Reegs isn't giving Looks, she's giving books. She stops for a moment in the hallway and gives me both.

Her Look says I Know It's Been a Hard Start of the Year and I Know Why.

The book is bright blue with a yellow stick-figure girl and a star on it.

I can't help myself; I reach out and take it. It feels cool and smooth in my hand.

I ask what I always ask: "What's it about?"

Mrs. Reegs answers the way she always does. With just a few words. "It's about...being."

"Being?"

She nods. Mrs. Reegs never explains why she's giving a book. She just wants everyone to figure it out for themselves. She's been this way since way back when she was our elementary school librarian. S and L and L and I had our very own book club, and for years, she'd bring four copies of whatever we were reading. She'd have to borrow from other libraries so we could each have our own. By the end of last year, she was only getting two.

And now...she doesn't have to worry about getting more than one.

There is this thing I do when I'm deciding about a book. Waiting to see if I'll connect with it. If I'll feel that *bah-bump* in my chest. First, I look at the cover. If I like the cover, I'll open the book and read the inside flap. If I like the inside flap, I'll read the first sentence. Then the first paragraph and the first page.

I do like the cover.

And the first sentence.

And the rest.

The edges of the hall sort of fade away.

I smile and keep reading.

It's about being....

After a few pages, I look up. "What do you mean, *it's about being*? Doesn't everybody...be?"

Mrs. Reegs just smiles. And holds open the door to the *Broadside* office. I didn't even notice we were here. She always says I'm the only person she knows who can walk and read at the same time without ever bumping into anything. When I asked if this meant I was a weirdo, she said no. It meant that even when I wasn't looking, I had something inside me that just knew the way to go.

I look at the *Broadside* door and hesitate.

When my mom says that thing about whatever you're feeling inside coming out, she's talking about her art. That's why all her paintings are big and beautiful and brave. They show what she's like on the inside.

But I have nothing inside that wants to come out right now. Especially not poetry from my heart for the whole school to read.

But Mrs. Reegs is still holding open that door.

So there is no choice for me but to go in. Having no idea what will come out.

Chapter 5

There are certain places that have something in the air. A sort of energy or mood to them, and no matter how long you stay away, you'll always remember what it felt like the first time you were there. Like the Wall on our path. Or my parents' art studio.

Or here. In the *Broadside* office.

There's something different about the light in here. It doesn't have that harsh, too-bright, headache-y feel like most of the classrooms in school do. I look around.

All the ceiling lights are off, and there are lamps on the tables and in the corners. A piece of paper is taped above the light switches. It says DO NOT CHANGE LIGHTS.

Pieces of antique furniture are everywhere: a dark wooden filing cabinet with brass handles, an old-fashioned typewriter with a leather case, one of those shelves on the wall made up of a printing drawer filled with blocks of letters with ancient ink still on them. Everything around us feels calm and warm and soothing and worn. As if it's all been here forever.

"Wonderful, aren't they?"

I nod.

"Briggs brought them in." Mrs. Reegs smiles toward a tall, skinny boy across the room. He's wearing a hat that he's pushed up so he can inspect the side of a small wooden table. "He and his grandfather used to travel to flea markets and restore the pieces they bought. He's handy, that one. I think I'd trust him to fix just about anything. He rewired all those old lamps by himself."

"Why do you only have the lamp lights on?" I ask.

"Well…we like this room to have a certain feel. And energy." I nod. I already know what she means. "I think people are most creative when they're...relaxed and calm and at peace. I like to think of the *Broadside* office as the Zen center of the school."

I believe her.

There's something about this place that...hums.

It hums and vibrates in a way that feels alive and steady and living and *there*. I don't know how else to explain it. There's something in here that makes my heart start counting out the beats of words that I already know will fall perfectly on my fingertips.

> *the air in here hums*
> *and the humming tells me this:*
> *people creating*

Five, seven, five. Haiku. I open my eyes. I'm still standing at the entrance with my hand on my chest. Mrs. Reegs is waiting patiently, and before I can shove my hands back into my pockets, she smiles and her Look says Ready? I take a deep breath and nod as she guides me in.

The *Broadside* office is in the large classroom off the Hub, where everyone can spread their work out and it's easy for Mrs. Reegs to oversee, since she's the teacher advisor and a librarian. The Hub is what she calls the library. I used to think she meant Hub like it was her Hubby, because she's so in love with it. But she explained it meant the Hub of Information. Then I found out that she was getting a divorce and felt really bad, but she said not to worry. It's been two years now, but everyone still calls her Mrs. Reegs even though she's not a Mrs. anymore. It's just hard to change something you're used to.

"Briggs," Mrs. Reegs calls out, but he's walking in the opposite direction and doesn't hear her. "When he slows down, I'll introduce you. Briggs is the editor in chief of the middle school section.

"We share the space with the main newspaper run by the high school kids. They're not as great at the Zen thing, but we're working on it. We do our best to keep them out on the days we're here." I notice that her eyes trail over to a corner where a boy in a striped shirt is working at a beautiful old steel desk. I wonder if the older kids are rough on the antiques. "They're a little more rambunctious and . . . we like a regular routine here," she says. "It just works better for us that way. Anyway, why don't we work our way around the room and I'll introduce you."

I look around, and I don't recognize anyone. Not only are they all eighth graders, but they obviously came from the other elementary schools in town. I put my hair behind my ears. Then pull it out. Then tuck it back again. I hope I don't have any leaves tangled up in there from lying on the grass out by the path.

As we walk up, this really pretty black girl smiles and pulls her headphones off. They're big comfy ones like mine, but hers are hand-painted on the sides. I wonder if she did it herself. Her music's so loud, I can tell she's listening to this song S and I loved when we were little. We called it the "Strange Train Song" because we thought the words were "Ch-ch-ch-choo-choo! Time to change your train—to the strange train!"

"Bea, this is Jaime. She and Briggs grew up at Westside Elementary together. She left us and spent last year at Hill on the Harbor Preparatory, but we're glad she's back."

"Hey, Bea," Jaime says.

I see the Hill Prep kids walking around town all the time. They have to wear blazers and these plaid skirts. Jaime has on a vintage concert tee with a skirt and these really cute boots. She doesn't seem like the uniform type.

"Jaime does our weekly online comic strip. Anaya,

here, is our short story editor, and sweet Tami McGee assists in all areas possible. And they're all avid readers. Look what I just gave Beatrix, girls." She points to the book I still have in my hands.

I force myself to smile, even though I know what Mrs. Reegs is doing. I want to tell her to stop. You can't just replace one...book group...with another.

I try to clear my throat, but nothing comes out. So I just sort of wave.

The girls nod and say, "Hi!" and then Jaime says, "I lo-oved that book. Good one, Mrs. Reegs! Hey, Bea, what are you listening to?" She is gesturing to the headphones around my neck. "I kind of have this epic song search going on and I need suggestions. Let me know if you want to listen in." I see she has a splitter, too, but not a bunny one like mine.

I tuck my phone deeper into my pocket with one finger so no one sees. How do I explain that I wear headphones all day and have a bunny splitter and a playlist set to go at a moment's notice, but I haven't listened to any music since the first day of school? Luckily, Mrs. Reegs is still moving along, so I just sort of shrug like *Oh, sorry, better keep going.*

As we walk away, I peek back over my shoulder.

Sometimes when I meet people, I like to imagine how my dad would draw them as superheroes. His latest graphic novel has this really cool Taiwanese superhero, and he always draws her with strong black lines and swooshing hair. She's an exact combination of him and my mom put together: goofy and kind like him and strong and brave like her.

Jaime has the kind of hair that's made up of about a zillion eensy little spirals. I know my dad would use one of his micro-pens and draw every single one. Her eyes are so dark, he'd do that trick where you paint a little white dot in them to show how they shine. She could get her superpower from her headphones. Or maybe from just one song. I wonder what's on that epic song search list of hers. I have a really epic song I love. Maybe she knows it.

I realize I've turned my head all the way around to stare like a weirdo and quickly look away.

Mrs. Reegs points and says, "These two over here handle all the art direction and layout. Todd and Janey, this is Bea, our poetry editor." They wave at me.

"Briggs!" she calls softly. But he says, "One sec, Mrs. Reegs." And disappears again.

I look around. There's one person I haven't met yet. The boy in the striped shirt, sitting at the old steel desk. His corner of the room is protected by an extra wall that's glass on top and solid on the bottom, so he kind of looks like an exhibit at the aquarium. He's bent over, concentrating on whatever complicated thing it is he's drawing. I can't see his face, but his hair is sandy and short and the back of his pale neck has a little red flush to it.

"Bea!" Mrs. Reegs calls me back before I can decide if he'd make a good superhero or not. She's headed the other way, where Briggs has finally come to a stop. His hat is the kind that grown-up men wear. A fedora. My dad would definitely do some kind of old-school Clark Kent thing with Briggs. His nose is so straight and strong, I think my dad would need a ruler to get it right.

"Briggs is probably one of the nicest people you'll ever meet," Mrs. Reegs whispers. "Nothing can stop that boy from smiling—Briggs! This is Bea."

Briggs turns toward me. And stops smiling.

The stack of paper he's holding falls to the ground.

Except that paper doesn't really fall. It swoops and swooshes and slides all over the floor. Falling paper likes to be as dramatic as possible.

"I'm sorry!" I say.

I drop down and try to gather as much as I can. Mrs. Reegs and Briggs join me.

Briggs looks up. "Don't be sorry. It's not your fault. You just surprised me."

"I'm sorr—" I start to say again. But he's right. What did I do? I'm not sure, but I'm sorry it happened. Then I think: Wait. What's so surprising about me?

I look around and people are sort of glancing over, but when they see it's just paper on the floor, they go back to work.

Only one person in the room is still watching. The boy in the striped shirt is observing us like we're the ones who are fish at the aquarium. But by the look on his face, maybe boring fish.

Briggs looks at me again. "Wait, who are you?"

Who am I?

Me?

"I'm...just Bea."

"Bea." Briggs stops picking up paper. "Beatrix Lee.

You did those painted poems. Like that spiral-y one with the cloud things—" Then he closes his eyes and says in one long breath,

Only the blue balloons know
that to scribble away
in the meltingly sun
and swimmingly swish
in the bristly sky
is one becoming
and becomingly one
and faraway near
when near far it comes
and botherly those
who bother to bother
and only the blue balloons know.

Then he takes a big gulp of air, lets it out, and grins at me.

I can't move. I just sit there on the floor, clutching paper to my chest. Did that just happen? Did an eighth grader—an eighth grader I've never even met before— quote one of my poems back to me?

I look at Mrs. Reegs and she's beaming.

Briggs continues, "And you were at that pool party the last weekend of summer, right?"

Oh no.

"You're the girl who—"

I stand and turn to Mrs. Reegs. "May I go to the bathroom, please?" I try not to let my hands shake as I hold out the papers I picked up off the floor.

She takes them, then studies my face for a second. "Sure, Bea. Is—is everything okay?"

I nod and force a smile. "Mmm-hmm. Be right back."

Then I walk out. Fast, but not too fast.

I don't want to see which Look she's giving me right now, and I definitely don't want her to see mine, which would be something like:

No, I'm Not the Girl from the Pool Party Because I Haven't Been the Same Person Since That Day.

Chapter 6

Every year on the last Saturday before school started, S would have an awesome End of Summer pool party. It was just S and L and L and me, but S's mom would get us stacks of pizza and do a make-your-own-sundae bar, and we'd swim and splash all day. The best part was that we'd each plan and decorate a secret surprise T-shirt to arrive in. We looked forward to that party all summer.

Only, this summer, my mom and dad and I went to Taiwan with my favorite aunt and uncle, who were teaching there for the year. My cousins, Tay and Lia, are nine and ten, but we always feel like we're the same age when we're together. Every single day, my parents and I explored the cities and saw tons of art. I learned how to order the best food at the night markets. I figured out how to ride the underground trains.

It was the best summer of my life.

And the funny thing is that even with all those amazing places we went to and all the things I got to see, my very favorite day was the one we spent just hanging out at the house my aunt and uncle were staying in. Because that was the day my parents taught me how to dive.

Of course, I knew how to swim and I had always loved just jumping off the diving board, but going in headfirst had always felt too scary and crazy and impossible. But that one day, we were all at the pool, and my aunt and my mom were playing this song from a concert they had front-row seats to years ago, and we were all dancing around and laughing and jumping and so happy and just like that, I announced that I wanted to dive.

Everyone cheered and, one by one, dove in to show me how. When it was my turn, I stepped up to the edge of the diving board and stood there, until my mom splashed at me from the deep end and shouted, "It's just like life, Trix! You can sit on the side or dive in!" And then my dad, who loved to show off how he could tread water just using his legs and kicking hard, held his arms way out to me and yelled, "You can do it! Go, go, go!"

I laughed. The water was so blue and sparkling. I was warm and buzzy from the sun and the music and the dancing and everyone around me, and so I took a big breath and did it. Badly. I got water in my nose, but then I got up and I did it again.

And again and again.

And then better and better until I never wanted to stop.

That night, I was humming and happy until I suddenly realized that I'd hardly talked to S all summer. I'd been so busy since we got to Taiwan, and S only has this flip phone that's about a hundred years old, so she never has good texting or reception. I had sent a bunch of postcards when I first got there. And we'd emailed once or twice, but then she left for sleepaway camp with L and L and I got busy and it was strange how during the best summer of my life, we were barely in touch.

We came back from Taiwan a few days before the pool party. I knew that L and L had started hanging out with A a little bit at the end of last year, but I didn't think it was that big a deal. L and L were best friends. And S and I were best friends. And the four of us did almost everything together, but we also did things with just the two of us sometimes. It didn't mean anything.

I knew they'd be there for the pool party just like every year. That pool party was *us*.

I didn't tell anyone we were back, because I wanted it to be a surprise.

I spent a whole day making the best End of Summer T-shirt of all time with tiny secret pockets sewn into the back and the words FREE TO BE YOU AND ME! in glittery fabric inks all over the front. It was the name of our favorite song from kindergarten, and we never started a summer party without blasting it at full volume. Our teacher had been playing it the first day we all met, and that made it the first song that was important to us as an Us.

For a song to be important, really and truly and

epically important, it has to be so many things. It has to make you want to laugh and dance, or it has to touch your heart in a way that you know—you just *know*—that something inside you has changed from the first moment you hear it.

The day of the party, I couldn't wait. I took the path to S and L and L's street, tiptoed to S's backyard, and hid my flip-flops by the fence. I couldn't hear any splashing, but there were voices murmuring and music was playing. Some dumb station, the kind I never let S listen to when I was around. But it was okay if they weren't playing our song, because I was bringing it! I started singing as loud as I could as I ran through the backyard, then burst through the gate, belting out the chorus at the top of my lungs, "Free to BEEEEE you and MEEEEEEE!"

Across the patio! Onto the diving board! Step-step—go! Not only was it the first dive my friends would ever see me do, it would be a dive like no other because when I hit the water—

Red!

Orange!

Yellow!

Green!

Blue!

Violet!

Every color of the rainbow flew behind me like underwater wings! Those secret pockets I'd sewn into the back of my shirt were filled with colored bath bombs. I wasn't just diving into Life, I was diving into everything! Being twelve! Seventh grade! The year we'd been dreaming of forever! As I flew through the water, I knew from the tips of my outstretched fingers to the bottoms of my pointed toes that I had never felt so completely like my own true self before and that I never wanted to feel any other way.

I pushed off the bottom like a rocket and burst into the air with my arms wide.

"It's—me!" I was shouting and laughing and trying to breathe all at the same time.

Nothing but that same music playing.

Was anyone out here? Should I have checked first?

I wiped the water out of my eyes and looked up.

I definitely should have checked.

A huge crowd of seventh-grade kids was standing

there, staring. I didn't even recognize half of them. There were eighth graders, too. Friends of S's brother, Jay. And all these grown-ups. I saw S's aunt and uncle from Texas. And her grandparents. What were they doing here?

S was standing in a foursome with A and L and L. Not one of them in a surprise End of Summer T-shirt. They were all in pretty dresses. S was twisting her hands together.

A few people kind of laughed. One person stood up and clapped loud and long. Then everyone just went back to talking. I didn't know what to do. I made my way to the shallow end and looked over at S.

A was asking, "Did your mom make you invite her?"

S didn't answer.

She didn't turn to A and say, "Are you kidding? She's my best friend in the world. Who invited you?" She didn't say anything. Just turned and walked into the house. I stood there a moment longer, then splashed out after her.

There was this strange pause as we both stood in her living room.

"You're back...." she mumbled.

I folded my arms in front of me and held myself tight. "Sorry. I just wanted to surprise you guys. What are all these people doing at our party?"

S looked down at the floor. "It's not *our* party. Jay wanted to have people from his class, and Mom said I should have the seventh graders we didn't know from Westside and Laurel Hollow, and since she got engaged—"

"Engaged!" I jumped up and down. It was what we'd been hoping and planning forever! So we could be bridesmaids. Not flower girls, bridesmaids. With matching dresses and everything! "Who—"

There was a sound and I looked up and saw S's mom standing there.

Holding hands with A's dad.

"Bea!" She came running over and gave me a big hug. "How was summer? I can't wait to hear about Taiwan! We missed you!"

"It was the best summer of my life!" I said. I glanced at S. Even as the words came out, I felt bad. But it was true. "Congratulations on your engagement!" I hugged her again.

Then A stepped up next to her dad.

"You got something on you," she said to S's mom.

She was in a white sundress, and my T-shirt had smudged her in so many different colors that they had turned into a pukey brown.

"I'm so sorry!" I said. "It won't stain—it's just bath bombs. It won't hurt the pool, either. I checked."

S's mom was looking down at her dress. "Don't even worry about it, I'm sure it will come right out—but Bea, let's get you off the rug." And I saw that the pukey brown color was running down my legs and all over the floor.

A's dad took a tiny step back as a little stream of water headed for his shiny shoes. He mumbled something about getting a towel and rushed off.

S's mom put a hand on my shoulder and looked me in the eyes. "You know, I have too many dresses anyway. This just gives me a chance to change and show another one off. Okay?"

I forced myself to nod. She gave me a quick smile and hurried away.

A looked me up and down, then finally shrugged. "I guess I'll see if I can help." And left.

S just stood there.

She didn't say, "It's so weird that I have to hang out with A now!"

She didn't say, "I have so much to tell you!"

Instead, she just stood there, twisting her hands, and then A was back. "Our parents need us. They're going to take pictures right after your mom changes."

I wanted to ask S what had happened. What was going on. I could feel the words building up inside me, but they wouldn't come out. I willed A to leave. But she stayed.

S said, "Okay," to A ...

... and then, after turning away ...

"See you later," to me.

The thing about words like *See you later* is that they don't really tell you how late later is actually going to be.

I didn't call the next day. I was too busy staring at my phone, wondering why *she* didn't call *me*. School was starting in three days. Maybe I would give her time. Our fights have always gone the same way since kindergarten:

We don't talk, we don't talk, we don't talk, then one of us hands the other a peace offering...

...and, just like that, it's over. But was this even a fight? Is it a fight when no one really says anything?

That day, I made a playlist.

It was filled with songs that said all the things I wanted to say to S. About friendship. About happiness. About believing in yourself.

I especially wanted her to listen to this girl-power song my cousins had played all summer long. We had memorized the words and would shout them and act them out and dance around the room late at night till our parents would wake up and, instead of yelling at us, would join in. I wanted S to hear those words. I imagined we'd use my bunny splitter and listen together and then sing them out into the universe just like my cousins did. I didn't want A to try and turn S into someone else. She was already someone. She was my best friend.

But then the first day of school came.

And I waited.

I waited by the path and the Wall with my song and my headphones and my bunny splitter. I jumped at every snapping twig and rustling bush. But it was never S. I waited so long that I was late for the first day of seventh grade.

I finally texted, **where are you.**

There was no answer for the longest time and then, **at school got ride.**

By the time I burst into Mr. Clarke's class, S was already sitting with A and L and L, and the only seat left was on the opposite side of the room, so I took it. Just as Mr. Clarke announced that we should all get used to where we were sitting because those were our assigned seats for the year. When I looked over to S, she wouldn't look up.

It's our only class together. It's been weeks now and I can't help it. Every day, I find myself waiting by the Wall. Just in case. And the words and the questions inside me keep building and building. But they never come out.

Chapter 7

I leave the *Broadside* and Briggs and all the papers on the floor behind me. Mrs. Reegs thinks I need to go to the bathroom, but that's only half true.

I just need to go.

Home.

I should have known after Social Studies Colon Ancient Civilizations that things weren't going to get any better. This day has been too much. Dad is away on one of his tours, but Mom will write me a note if I ask, no problem. I slip out the side exit and manage to get back to the path behind the school and follow it along until I come to the opening by our backyard. I don't think I even take a breath until I step onto our grass and look up at my parents' studio.

It was a big empty barn before they turned it into their perfect workspace. Mom's side takes up most of it since all her work is large, and I mean huge. There are giant canvases leaning up against all the walls, and they keep getting bigger and bigger. So I understand why I don't have my own art corner here anymore; my mom really needs the space. Dad doesn't mind. He says all he needs is a small desk and to be able to look up and see her.

My dad's graphic novels have a pretty serious following. People line up at comic book conventions to see him, and they dress like the characters from his books. Especially the new Taiwanese superhero in her rainbow cape and combat boots.

When Dad was first creating her, he asked Mom and me what we thought the best superpower was. And then what its weakness would be. Like, Superman is super-strong and can fly, but he can be defeated by kryptonite.

My mom, of course, said Art was the best super-power because it can take what only exists in someone's imagination and make it real.

Dad laughed but then ended up using her idea. He named his hero Sky, and she has the ability to draw things that come to life. Like weapons or a shield or a dragon to fly away on, and, of course, really funny stuff, too, like flying pork dumplings to hit her enemy in the face.

I wish I had helped my dad that day. I had all these ideas, but I couldn't decide what to say and I didn't want to choose wrong and have them think their daughter didn't get the creativity gene. And Dad was so in love with Mom for her answer and they had started kissing and laughing so much that I just left.

Sky's weakness is that if she ever loses her rainbow cape, she becomes powerless. Which is pretty good, though I think if he asked me now what her kryptonite should be, I'd say invisible ink. Because Sky has the power to take the ideas in her head and draw them to make them real, but invisible ink can make those ideas disappear before they even have a chance to be seen.

There are these people who want to make Dad's

book into a movie, so he has been traveling a lot lately. It's so, so exciting, but I feel as if I barely get to see him at all.

I close my eyes when I enter our backyard, wondering what I'll see when I look toward the wide windows of the studio. Will it be the back of my mom, holding her shoulders in a way that means she should not be interrupted? Or will it be—

I hear knocking on glass and my heart leaps and there she is. Waving and beckoning through the window. Paint-splattered and so blissfully happy, my heart hurts.

I run to the studio doors. Before I go in, I take a breath and try to rearrange my face, but I'm not sure where all the pieces go. My mouth feels all wrong. My nostrils are too flared. I'm sure my brows are pulled together too tight. I rest my hand on the door. The handle is old and brass and shaped like a dragon, clinging to the wood with its claws. It takes jiggling, but then it opens.

She must have had a really good day of painting.

Well, a good day and night and morning. I don't think she came back into the house last night, which means she probably didn't sleep. She doesn't even notice that I should be in school right now. She's just smiling and glowy as she waves me in.

She has no idea there's a streak of blue paint on that spot she rubs on her forehead when she's deep in thought. My dad calls her new series of paintings her Blue Phase.

I rush across the room and hug her tight. I grab the folds of her long skirt and hold on, wondering how much time I have.

She squeezes me tight, then tighter, and I think of all the colors I'll be smudged with when she lets go. Indigo. Steely blue. The color of the sky. She kisses me deeply on each cheek. "Mmmm-mmmmm. How was your day, Trix? Anything—" She places her hand over her chest and gives a soft drum, *bah-bump bah-bump?*

My heart fights with my face. I had *bah-bump* moments to tell her about every day in Taiwan, but not since school started. Luckily, I know exactly how to distract her.

I force a little laugh. "I want to hear about your day

first. What colors did you paint today? Blue, blue, or blue?"

It works.

She laughs and rumples my hair. "Well…" and her attention shifts, exactly as I knew it would. Without a second's worry. "Tina called from the gallery again to find out how everything is coming. I still didn't tell her I stopped doing abstracts and started the whole self-portrait thing, because you know she hates those…. But I had to do what I feel…. Don't you love this blue?"

I look up at the ten-foot painting of my blue mom, naked except for a cloud or two, and floating through a strange sky filled with planets and swimming with celestial fish. Her pregnant belly is round and filled with tiny stars and jeweled birds. I love it. But I think I'd love anything she did, just because it's always so…her.

"Which reminds me: middle name time. When am I going to hear what you've chosen for your baby sister? Little Starling is going to be here before you know it…."

I pause. I've been the only child for twelve years, and my parents have been trying forever to have another baby, so I know it's this huge honor to choose a middle name for her, but what if I choose wrong?

I cling tighter to Mom's skirt. "I don't know yet, but I love the blue. I do...."

"I love the blue, too." She pulls me back into a hug. "And you."

Oh.

...I love the blue, too. And you...

I don't say it out loud, but Mom can tell. She gives me a gentle push toward the door. "I know that face.... Run along now and make me a poem, my poet. I love you...."

I try to hold on to her skirt for just a moment longer, but as she turns, it slips from my fingers. And then just like that, she's back in the blue and there's nothing to do but leave.

The dragon door clicks shut behind me, and I stand outside the studio for a moment, holding my hand to my heart, feeling my fingers count the beats.

I love the blue, too,
and you...and you—oh, I love
the blue, too, and you...

I close my eyes and imagine the words drawn loose and loopy in indigo ink speckled with stars. But when I open my eyes again and see my raised hand etching curls into the air, I stop. Even if I rushed off this second to find paper and pen and ink, Mom is already floating off somewhere in her blue painterly world, and I don't know if there's a way back in.

I leave the words hanging in the air behind me and walk away.

Chapter 8

A few years ago, I was in my bedroom, figuring out a poem in the air, when I opened my eyes to see my mom standing there in the doorway, watching me and smiling. She was holding one of her paint pens. She slipped it into my still-raised hand and then led me forward until it touched the nearest wall.

Maybe in another house, another kid might not know what to do, but this was me and it was my mom and our house, and I didn't hesitate for a second. I wrote the words out right there on my bedroom wall in big swooping script. I let the flourishes turn into sweeping swirls and beasts and birds and then back into words again. I colored them in, filling the spaces with the ways I was feeling. If I wasn't sure what to write next, I'd close my eyes and write in the air until I knew.

My mom left her entire collection of pens with me, and when she brought my dad in later that afternoon to look, he said, "So this is what the inside of your head looks like." Which made my mom hug him and kiss him about a hundred times on the cheeks until they were both laughing like crazy, and then they linked arms and headed back to their studio together.

I used up every inch of my walls and even the inside of my closets, the skinny strips of the windowsills, and the big, wide width of the ceiling. I took pictures of all my favorite bits and pieces. And those pictures are what I sent to Mrs. Reegs last spring when I applied for the job of middle school poetry editor for the *Broadside*. The editors of the middle school paper are always eighth graders, but when I stood in the middle of my room, surrounded by all my colors and words, I felt like I could do anything.

What you feel inside is what you put out in the universe.

After the first week of school, all I could feel inside was that I wanted to paint over it all.

When I had asked my parents, Mom looked like she wanted to cry.

I knew she would react that way, and I remember thinking hard about how my face should look for this conversation. I remember thinking about how Mom liked to hear things and what sorts of ideas she responded to the best.

"I took pictures of everything already," I said, holding up my phone. "And I was just thinking how it was the beginning of … a whole new part of my life and that I wanted to start free and fresh for … for middle school and if I made my walls white, it would be like … blank paper. You know, for this next—new—beginning." I even threw my arms wide as if to embrace all the possibilities that blank paper could offer.

Mom's eyes sparkled. She grabbed me and swung me around and danced with me in a circle till we were both laughing and I had almost forgotten what we were talking about.

"You are so my daughter," she said, hugging me close and kissing me three times on each cheek. Over the next few days, she brought me several samples of white paint. Some that looked like stark white paper. Some like linen-y fabrics. Some like textured drawing paper. She painted large loose swatches, scribbling down the name of each paint next to it, and told me to watch what they did as the sun moved across the room. To take my time and choose the white that most spoke to me.

I chose the one that seemed the thickest.

Mom drove right into town to pick everything up. Two gallons of paint, a pan, a roller, and a drop cloth have been sitting on the floor in my room for three weeks now. I just haven't quite been able to start.

Till today.

I carefully spread the drop cloth. Pry a can of paint open and stir it up. I like the way a paint roller makes it easy. It picks up just the right amount of paint and covers whatever you need to cover.

I take a last look at my walls. They're just words. It's not the end of the world.

Maybe it *is* a fresh start and a blank page, and all those things I was saying to my mom are actually true.

I bet by the time I count five strokes of paint, I will already feel better.

Deep breath.

One...So I caused a scene in Mr. Clarke's class. From now on, I'll be so quiet that no one will know I'm there.

Two...So I made Briggs, the fix-it boy, drop paper all over the *Broadside* office. I bet it's all picked up now.

Three...The pool party was weeks ago. The colors in the water are long gone.

Four...And today was today and tomorrow will be different.

Five...I'll start this whole beginning of middle school over again.

I blink hard and steady my roller. Why not? It'll be great. Really, really great. Because if you think about it, what is a blank page, anyway? It's a place where just about anything can happen.

Chapter 9

Today is the blank page day.

Anything can happen.

After I finished painting my walls last night, the fumes were so strong, I had to sleep on the sofa downstairs instead of in my room. So the day's already started out differently than before.

As I pass the clearing by our Wall, I look straight ahead and I don't pause for even a second. If I keep walking, I won't stop and wait, and if I don't wait, I won't be late for Social Studies Colon Ancient Civilizations for the first time this year. And that will definitely be something new. So today, no waiting in the place where no one ever shows up.

But sometimes paths have their own ideas. A sudden flash of color that disappears around the turn ahead makes me stumble. Because I know that color. I'd know that orange-y red anywhere. It's the color of S's favorite sweater. We bought it together last year. She got red. I got blue.

My heart is pounding as I walk fast. And then faster. Then break into a run.

Wait, wait, wait, wait—

"Wait—!" I cry out as I make the turn.

And almost run right into Briggs. "Oh! Hey, Bea!"

I look past him to one side and then the other.

"Are you okay?" he asks.

We're closer to the school now. Other kids are merging onto the main path. Several red and orange sweaters and jackets go by. Even Briggs's backpack is orange-y red.

What was I thinking? Why would S even be at our Wall when she hasn't spoken to me in weeks? When she probably still drives in with A every day?

"Bea?"

Briggs is still here. Standing in front of me.

"I…" I shake my head. "…forgot…something." I pause for a moment and then just turn and head back.

"Oh, okay.…" I hear him answer. "Better hurry! Don't be late!"

I keep walking.

The freshly painted surface of this day suddenly feels like it's been smeared with all the things I can't change. Because the truth is that you can't start over. You can't take things back or turn them into something else just because you want to. The world doesn't work that way. If it did, I'd take it all back. Everything. Every bit of color on that silly T-shirt at the pool party. Every second of that stupid dive in the pool. I'd take back every bit of every moment when I was crazy enough to let a piece of myself loose out there in the world. If only I—

I run to the Wall.

I'm going to take back my invisible haiku. I know it won't change anything, but it's the one thing I can do. I know it won't stop the fact that S and L and L and me is now S and L and L and A. But I still want to do it. I have to.

I push my face up to the Portal, but it is dark beyond dark and I can't see anything.

I try to shove my hand in, but the hole's too small.

I look on the ground for a stick and find one long and thin enough to fit with some wiggle room. If I put my heart out in the universe, shouldn't I be allowed to take it back? It takes me a few minutes, but I finally hear the barely there crunch of paper and manage to drag it out.

The grass tie is gone. It must've come undone. I unroll the paper.

And then stare.

Because it's not my poem. It's not my invisible haiku.

It is not five words
(I mean syllables) and then
seven and then five.

It looks like...someone has written back.

Chapter 10

```
Hi.
```

Bah-bump. Bah-bump. Bah-bump.

My heart is beating so loud, I look around to see if anyone has heard, but there are no rustling bushes or snapping twigs or sudden flashes of color at the turn of the path. It's just the Wall, the Portal, and me.

```
    I'm glad you left matches. I
was'n't sure what they were for,
```

but then I saw the blank paper and
how it wasn't quite smooth, and I
figured it out. Invisible ink! At
first I was confused, because you
wrote about blind <u>allies</u>, but I
think you mean blind <u>alleys</u>. Allies
is the plural of "ally" and ally
means someone who's there for you.
Like a friend. So a "blind ally"
would be like a friend who couldn't
see they were there for you! I think
you mean a blind alley from a maze.
Like a dead end.

   You said you wonder why they're
there. I know why. Blind alleys mean
you're going the wrong way. They're
there so you can turn around and
try something else. Something even
better. I hope you write again. It's
nice to have you there.

Stop.
This is the first thing I say to myself. Stop. Because

what I'm thinking is too big and too impossible and will hurt too much if it's not true.

Because this answer. *This answer.* I know in my heart and I know in my head and I know in every molecule of my brain that this answer is from S. It's her way of reaching out to me. And I cannot stop myself from listing the proof:

Her orange-y red sweater. I *did* see her. She was here when she left me this note.

She knows about invisible ink from our *Start Your Own Secret Club* book.

She knows that the Portal is not just some beetle-and-maybe-moss-filled hole. Who else would even know to look inside?

Her answer. This note. It's the end of our fight or whatever this whole thing has been during this time we haven't talked, and we haven't talked, and we haven't talked.

This is her peace offering, and now, it's all finally going to be over.

In the distance, I can already hear the first bell ringing up at the school. I clutch S's letter in my hand and run as fast as I can.

Chapter 11

I have to get there before the second bell rings. I have to get to Social Studies Colon Ancient Civilizations before class starts so that I can get to S and tell her I found the peace offering and I know it's her and that everything will be all right and we can start the year over.

The second bell rings as I take the last turn of the path.

I'm late.

I sprint for the main entrance and push through.

Why are the halls so long? It's not until I see the doors to Mr. Clarke's classroom closing that I realize I can't just crash into the room. I can't be too much, today of all days. Today I will not make a scene. I force myself to stop. I smooth my hair down and take a deep breath.

I quietly open the door and slip in.

As I head for my desk, Dan clutches his throat and pretends to cry, "*Nooo!*"

"None of that, Daniel-san," Mr. Clarke says. "Back in your seat. We have a lot to cover today. Though, Extra Credit Curveball to anyone who can tell me which iconic eighties movie the nickname 'Daniel-san' comes from!" He looks over at me and nods. "You take your seat, too, Miss Beatrix . . . *Belden?* Lee."

And that's that. Class begins.

S and L and L and A sit in their usual seats. S has her back to me the whole time and doesn't even glance my way, but if she did, she would see that I am the model of respectability. Back straight. Calm and listening. I don't clonk into anyone or write in the air.

And I don't hear a single word Mr. Clarke says because I spend the entire time wondering how to get S alone. I think the best thing to do is find her during lunch, when we can really talk. After class, I'll leave quickly before Dan can say anything to me and cause a scene. I don't want S to see me be part of any more scenes. Then all I have to do is get through a few more classes till lunch.

I won't be sneaking off to the Wall today. I'm going to walk into the cafeteria to find S. This whole time, I've been so afraid she wouldn't sit with me, but now I realize I didn't even give her a chance to choose. I made the choice for her. I never even showed up.

But today, I'm going.

We'd been talking about eating lunch in the middle school cafeteria since we were in second grade. It was going to be the first time we could eat pizza and french fries with money we brought ourselves, instead of the prepaid meal plan our parents set up.

The rest of my morning classes are a blur.

At lunch, I stand outside the cafeteria door for a moment and prepare myself. I already know where the girls will be sitting. The round table under the big window. It has sunlight and it's not too close to the lunch line, so you can hear each other when you talk. We snuck in last year and tried sitting at all the different tables and finally picked that one. I step inside. Even though it's crowded and noisy, I see them right away and keep my eyes on the back of S's head as I move toward them. I'll just ask her if we can talk for a second. I know her. She'll nod her head and jump up, and this whole terrible first month of school will be done.

A is sitting in the seat facing me. I don't think there's ever been a day she wasn't completely neat and tidy. All her clothes always match. Her short brown hair is always stick straight and neatly parted. And her nails are always painted and never chipped. I guess it's nice to always look so put together, but it probably takes an awful lot of work, too. I mean, when would you ever have time left over to draw or paint or write or do anything fun?

I'm walking straight toward A, but she doesn't see me. She's asking something in the kind of voice that people think is quiet but that carries all the way across a crowded cafeteria where your three former best friends are sitting at what was supposed to be your table.

"But what would you do?"

"If what?" S sounds nervous.

"If she wanted to sit here..."

I can barely hear S answer, "Who?"

A's voice always sounds bored. "That girl. The weird one from the pool party. The one who yelled in class. Wasn't she your friend in kindergarten or something?"

It's suddenly as if I'm in a movie scene and someone else is in control of the sound and lighting and they've dimmed the crowds and turned up the volume on S's voice even though she's only mumbling.

"She wouldn't...and she's not—she was—but—"

A shrugs. "She's kind of pretty and looks sort of normal....You'd never know..."

It's funny how you can change paths with just the slightest move. Your legs will keep walking even though you can't feel them anymore. You don't even have to be able to see past the blurring of your eyes.

I push my headphones back up on my head and my hands deep into my pockets. On the outside, I look like I was planning on heading for the exit this whole time. But on the inside, it feels like falling. I just hope I get out of here before the inside catches up with the outside and spills out onto my face and down my cheeks and turns into a river that fills everything.

I pass the table. L and L are talking in voices that

sound like background noise, A is picking through her french fries, and S is twisting her hands.

Don't see me. Don't see me. Don't see me.

If I could, I would pour lemon juice with three drops of water on myself until I disappear.

Chapter 12

The hallway feels like that path in the House of Mirrors that looks like it's getting smaller and smaller but at the same time never ends. Which can only mean that you're getting smaller and smaller, too.

The last students are filing into lunch or class. The hall will be empty soon. If a teacher finds me wandering alone, they'll send me back into the cafeteria.

And I can't go back and just sit at an empty table. I can't sit alone somewhere in the kind of room where proof exists that S could never be the one who sent me the note in the Portal. And I don't think I have the strength to run to the path now. Stealth or not.

For a second, I think about going to the Hub to see Mrs. Reegs, but she would start giving me Looks and wanting me to explain and express myself, and I haven't seen her since I walked out of the *Broadside* office yesterday to go to the bathroom and never returned. The last thing I want to talk about is why I never came back to her precious Zen center of the school.

I pause a moment and close my eyes....

> *the* Broadside *office*
> *with its low lights and calm hum.*
> *is it a safe place?*

There's always a sign hanging on the door that says THIS OFFICE IS CLOSED EXCEPT DURING OFFICIAL BROADSIDE MEETINGS. PLEASE DO NOT ENTER. And I know there's another sign when you walk inside that says PLEASE RESPECT EVERYONE ELSE'S SPACE. Mrs. Reegs spends an awful lot of time putting up signs in the *Broadside* office.

But I wonder if she actually locks it.

I give the hallway a quick glance and then reach one

hand out and try the door. It's open. I dart into the room and shut it behind me. My heart is pounding as I keep one eye pressed against the crack and wait to see if anyone has noticed.

Someone has.

"No one is supposed to come in here during lunch."

I give a yelp and spin around.

It's the boy. The boy in the striped shirt. In a different striped shirt.

"You scared me!" I say. "And wait, if no one's supposed to be here, why are *you* here?"

He shakes his head. "This is where I come during this time. Why are you here?"

"Does Mrs. Reegs know you're—"

"Fee gave me permission. Did she give you permission?"

"Who's *Fee*?"

"Ms. Rodriguez. Her name is Sofía. I call her Fee. Why are you here during lunch?"

"I—I don't know...."

"You don't know why you're here?" He stares down at his drawing as if the answer is there.

I don't know what else to say. Or if I should sit and ignore him and wait out the rest of the lunch period and then leave. I move toward a table that will keep his aquarium wall between us.

"You left yesterday," he says.

"What?"

"You were here for only a minute, and then you left after you made Briggs drop his papers."

"I didn't—" I stop. I did make Briggs drop his papers. And I did leave. "Well, there was just too much going on and I needed to get out. Don't you ever have days that are too much?"

He pauses for a moment. Like he's really thinking about it. "Yes," he says.

He begins drawing again. I think maybe our conversation is done, and I start to sit down when he says, "I know you."

I stand up again. "You do?"

"You're Beatrix Lee. You seem to be interested in masonry. Your parents are artists. We walk the same path."

"I've never seen you on my path—and what's masonry? Okay, wait—" It's too much information at once. "Just...tell me your name."

"Will. Masonry is the craft of stonework. The earliest known labyrinth was made from stone, but I prefer modern ones, which can be made of tall or short hedges or rock paths on the ground and are unicursal in design rather than multicursal."

I have no idea what he's talking about. But he doesn't seem to notice. He just keeps working on his drawing.

Something clicks. "You're Dan Ross's cousin." I remember Dan's mean comment that his cousin was weird. This, more than anything, makes me want to give this Will a chance. "You gave him that maze."

"I don't like mazes." He doesn't even bother to acknowledge his relationship to Dan, which makes me kind of like him.

I take a tiny step toward the edge of his wall and glance at his paper. "If you don't like mazes, why are you drawing one? And I think I saw you drawing one yesterday, too."

"I'm drawing a labyrinth, not a maze. That wooden maze was a gift from my aunt. She's like you. She doesn't know the difference, either. So I gave it back. This"—he studies his drawing—"is a labyrinth."

I think of the inside of my brain as a complicated filing system. There's something about Will that makes me think I don't have enough information in there. Dan

Ross had said the maze in class was a labyrinth. But I'm not going to trust him.

"Um, aren't they the same thing?" I ask. "Mazes and—and labyrinths, I mean."

Will continues to draw. "Most people think they are, and historically, the words were used interchangeably, but not anymore. The colloquial meaning of *labyrinth* is completely different."

I still don't understand and I kind of want to ask him what *colloquial* means, but I decide to look it up when I get home. If I can remember how to spell it. I think about the blind allies and blind alleys. Spelling is not my strength, but I bet it's Will's.

"According to modern definition, a maze has multiple paths with blind alleys and loops, but a labyrinth has a single path. You know exactly where to go in and exactly where to go out." He leans close to his drawing and inspects it. "That's the difference."

I think I get it. And I don't know why, but I'm thinking of Hammy and my heart gives a little *bah-bump.* "So there's no way to get lost or to go in the wrong direction or make a mistake if you're in a labyrinth like this?"

"No. It's impossible. I just told you: a labyrinth has a

single path. It winds and turns toward a center spot and then leads you back out the same way."

I lean over and stare at this...labyrinth. "Really..."

"People use modern labyrinths as a method of meditation. It's calming when you walk them."

I want to pull my hands out of my pockets and trace the path and see what it feels like to go all the way through without getting lost or stuck. "I like that. I like...having only one path...and never getting lost."

Will stops drawing. He's still looking down when he says, "This is the most I've ever heard you say. You don't talk a lot."

"When—where have you ever heard me not talking?" Does that even make sense?

"We're in two classes together. You just don't see me. Most people don't, because I'm better at observing than being observed. It's a good way to get information."

"Information—about what?" I ask.

"Anything. Anything you need to figure out. It all comes down to gathering all the information you can, making a list, and then drawing conclusions."

drawing conclusions...

Oh. I like the way that sounds. I like that conclusions can be drawn. And they're something you need to figure out. So it sounds sort of like you can figure things out with art.

draw-ing-con-clu-sions (five)

I open my eyes with a start and put my hands back in my pockets. I look over at Will, but he hasn't noticed. Or if he has, he doesn't say anything.

I clear my throat. I don't really need to; it's just in case he thinks it's been quiet for too long. "I...um, I like that."

"You already said that. Do you mean the same thing or something different?"

"I like...the phrase *drawing conclusions*." I sit down in a seat nearby. "And everything you were saying, you know, about the one path."

For a minute, I think either he hasn't heard me or he's ignoring me. Then he says, "Most people aren't interesting to talk to." He pauses and carefully extends a line in his drawing. "You are, though."

I stand back up. "Me? Why?"

He studies the new line and then nods. I guess it passes. "You don't like mazes, either."

I don't know how to respond at first. Then I think about Hammy and Dan Ross and Social Studies Colon Ancient Civilizations. He's right. I don't.

"But you like labyrinths." He says this the way he has been saying everything. As a statement.

I nod. "I do..."

I sit and eat my lunch, and Will keeps on drawing and we don't say another word for the rest of the time, but I think that's okay, because I've said more today to this boy in the striped shirt here in the Zen center of the school than I have in any of my classes all year. And for the first time since this summer, I have this funny feeling. I feel like maybe I belong somewhere.

I belong with the people who prefer labyrinths over mazes.

Chapter 13

On the way home, the path seems different and new. But also the same.

Because I know exactly where it leads.

And I like that.

It leads to the clearing by my Wall.

And then it leads home.

There are no decisions to make or dead ends to run into or monsters in the middle. I don't have to think about what happened in the cafeteria. I don't need to know who left me the note in the Portal because it doesn't matter.

I mean, it matters. But it doesn't matter who.

It's someone with a light.

And I want to write back.

I settle down by the Wall. Inside, I'm thinking about Will and the labyrinth and having one path. And I want to let the person who wrote to me know that there's a place where blind alleys don't exist. I pull out my favorite blue pen. Because this is not the kind of feeling that feels…invisible. This feels true and blue.

<u>the labyrinth</u>
following along
without any unknown turns
a clear path beckons

Do you know the difference between a maze and a labyrinth? A labyrinth has one path that leads in and then out. Don't you think following along a simple path like that is so much better? No blind alleys! (spelled right haha) Thank you for writing back. I'm glad someone else out there knows about invisible ink. Also, it doesn't really matter, but do you know who I am? You don't have to answer! I'm just curious.

From,

I pause. And then write:

Your Friend

I roll the tiny piece of paper up and tie it with a blade of grass. I look at the Portal. I tuck it in. No questions. No worries. It just feels right. I brush off my hands and follow the path that connects to the next path that takes me the rest of the way home.

Chapter 14

The next day, I do my best to pass by the Hub as quickly as possible whenever I'm walking down the hall.

It works. Until third period.

There's no mistaking the voice.

"Beatrix!"

I stumble in my panic.

"Bea!"

The sneakers appear. Today, blinding white with green laces and a black star on each side.

I look up at Mrs. Reegs and I don't quite recognize her Look.

"Hi. Do you have a minute to talk?" She leans over and holds open the door.

I open my mouth, but nothing comes out. I should've asked Mom to let me have a mental health day. She never says no. The best ones are when she surprises me in the morning by just yelling, "Time to go!" which means a whole day in the city for the three of us, looking through galleries and art stores and finding little secret places to eat. My parents don't really stress over school. My dad says there are many ways to be smart. Word Smart. Math Smart. Feelings Smart. Obviously, he and my mom are Art Smart. And, probably, Mushy in Love Smart, too.

I don't know what I am yet. But I definitely don't feel very Word Smart right now. I can't think of what to say to Mrs. Reegs. I'm just waiting for her to ask why I never came back from the bathroom.

Instead, she asks, "How do you like the book?"

Oh. "...I like it. I do. Actually, I really like it a lot. I read some in bed last night."

She smiles, because her favorite superpower is definitely finding the right books for the right people.

Like when S and L and L and I were afraid of the bullies at the playground in elementary school, and she handed us books about these kids who go to a magical land and help save the creatures there from a terrible witch.

Or the time when I was afraid to show my writing to anyone and she gave us a book about four sisters who were all so different, just like the four of us, and one of them was a writer who wasn't afraid to do big, bold things.

And last spring, when L and L didn't want to be in the book club anymore, she gave me and S this book about a girl who lived in a parallel world, where everyone had a special creature who was their best friend and soul mate and they could never be separated.

But I was the only one who read it. S said it was too hard and complicated. We never had a book club meeting for it. Then I left for Taiwan and now here we are.

Well, here I am.

Mrs. Reegs interrupts these thoughts. "I had a feeling you'd like it. It's pretty much a perfect novel."

Really? Mrs. Reegs doesn't usually say anything until we're done reading.

"What makes it so perfect?"

"Well, for me it's...how everything is connected. Even things like the porcupine necktie come full circle and are connected to everything else in a way that makes sense. Maybe not in the way you expect it to, but it still feels just...perfect."

I don't know what this means, but I nod anyway.

Mrs. Reegs pauses, then leans toward me. "I sent you a list of everyone's contact info from the *Broadside*. Just in case you ever wanted to talk about ideas with anyone...or for any other reason. You know, they all really like you. And your poetry. Especially our editor in chief."

Briggs liked one of my poems so much, he memorized it.

She smiles. "So, see you at the next meeting? You know the way."

I do.

Her Look says I Hope You Come.

I don't know what my Look says. But maybe I will.

Chapter 15

At lunch, I find myself heading back to the *Broadside* office. I peek both ways down the hall and then slip in. Will is in his usual place behind his aquarium wall at the big steel desk. Only today, he doesn't have a drawing in front of him. He has a slim silver laptop and a folder. I wonder if he'll badger me again about whether I have permission to be here.

Or maybe he'll be happy to see me.

"Hey..." I wave from the door. "Hi, Will."

He doesn't look happy. But he doesn't look annoyed

or mad or anything else, either. He just glances at his watch and says, "Hi."

I put my lunch down on a table that faces the open side of his corner. It's big enough for two people to sit and eat, side by side. I take a deep breath and let it out. "So...do you...do you want to come sit here and eat lunch?"

"No, I only like to sit here."

Oh.

I try again. "What are you looking at?"

"I'm reading an article."

I take a step toward him. I think carefully before I respond. I'm starting to see that I need to be very specific with Will to get the answers I want. "Okay, um, what I mean is: What are you reading about in the article?"

"I think I found my eleventh."

"Eleventh...what?"

"Labyrinth."

"Eleventh article about labyrinths?"

"The eleventh labyrinth that I will complete when I walk it on the eleventh day of the eleventh month."

Oh.

the eleventh day
the eleventh labyrinth
the eleventh month

Five, seven, five.

Haiku.

I open my eyes.

"I was thinking of doing it at eleven o'clock, but that might be inconvenient," he says.

"Eleven at night? Wouldn't that be scary? What if you get lost?"

Will pauses. "I told you yesterday. Labyrinths have a single path. There's only one way in and one way out. Even if it's dark, you can't get lost. They aren't scary; they're calming. And I was going to say that I was considering eleven at night, but that was before I found out that the eleventh is a Saturday. So I can go during the day. The other labyrinths I did were small ones. This is the first really big one. I want to be able to see it."

"Oh. I like that...."

"You like what? The same thing you said you liked yesterday? Or something else?"

"I meant I like the eleventh-labyrinth-on-the-eleventh-day-and-eleventh-month thing. It's poetic....I write poems," I offer. "And I was just thinking of a haiku, which is this kind of poem made of three lines with five syllables and then seven and five again, so you can't waste any words—"

"I need information on the Leland estate." He doesn't even look as if he heard me.

Okay. So, not into poetry. "You mean Mr. Leland with the mansion up on the Neck? He has, like, a famous maze."

"I know. And it's a labyrinth. Do you know him? Or anything about him? I've been collecting information since fifth grade, but it's very hard to find. This is what I have so far...." Will opens a folder and pulls out a piece of paper. A few other pieces fall out, and he has to scramble to get them.

"Why don't you use a spiral notebook?" I ask. "Then nothing would fall out."

"I don't like spiral notebooks. You can't change the order of the pages, and when you rip them out, the edges are all jagged and the tiny pieces of paper get stuck in the wire."

"But what if you—"

"ONE. Mr. Leland has a private residence in Cauffield State Park, which is the biggest state park on Long Island and one of the biggest in New York. The Lelands previously owned all the land on that part of the Neck and then sold most of it to the state, but they kept six hundred acres of property by the water for themselves.

"TWO. Leland Labyrinth is the third-biggest privately owned labyrinth in the country."

"Wow, the third-biggest—"

"THREE. Mr. Leland has no children and no one else has been allowed into the labyrinth since it was built. The builders did not have permission to take photographs. So no one outside his immediate family has ever seen it."

I look over at his piece of paper. "You're making a list."

"I told you yesterday. It's the best way to draw conclusions and then figure out a plan. Do you have anything to add to it?"

Oh, I really, really want to add something to the list. "Um, well, I know he's rich. I met him for, like, two seconds because he bought some of my mom's art for

103

the lobby of his office building in the city. Two of her famous abstract pieces."

Will goes back to his laptop and starts scrolling. I'm not a valuable source of information. He doesn't care about art in Mr. Leland's office building. He needs information about the labyrinth or the Leland estate.

"And...oh! The hounds! His property is guarded by these Killer Hounds."

At this, Will grabs a pencil. It's one of those mechanical ones that you click for the lead to come up. "I need to know more."

I have information!

"Well, they're supposed to be these, like, seriously scary huge dogs that have been trained on raw meat, and they guard the estate and—and—I heard once that Mr. Leland can see everything that goes on from this high tower and he has this red button he pushes when he wants to release the hounds from the dungeon."

Will skips over the part about the tower and dungeon. "Tell me what you mean by killer. Like they've killed in the past? Or they're trained to kill?"

"Oh, I—I actually don't know. That's just what everyone says."

Will adds *KILLER HOUNDS* to his list. "Dogs are hard to get past. I'll need to figure out where the property is vulnerable."

"Vulnerable?" I ask.

"Everything has a weakness."

I think of my dad and his superheroes. "It's true," I say. "Everything and everyone has a strength and a weakness."

Will pauses. He glances up at me for just a second, then looks down again. "Dogs are a strength. I just need to figure out what the weakness in their security system is, but I don't really think it'll be a problem."

"You don't?"

"I just need the right information. Then I can figure it out."

Oh, right. Information.

"But after you figure that out, you still have to get in, right? How will you do that?"

"I have to come up with a plan and follow it. This article says Mr. Leland does not allow visitors. So I'll figure out the weak spot on the property and get in, and whatever plan I come up with, I'll practice at least three times, and then I will be able to do it."

I hold up a hand. "Okay, wait. For someone who was giving me such a hard time about having permission to be somewhere, don't you think it's kind of intense to break into the most famous mansion on Long Island?"

"I have permission," he says.

"You do? But then why do you have to break in?"

"Mr. Leland's niece gave me permission when I wrote to her, and he tried to take it back. But I'm not going to recognize his authority, because the person I wrote to gave me permission."

"So you just decide for yourself which rules to listen to and which ones to break?"

He's quiet for a moment. Then he says, "Which rules are you listening to when you run out of school and go to the path in the middle of the day?"

I swing around to look at the windows across from him, and there's a direct view of the soccer field that leads to the path. He sits here for lunch every day. I sneak out during lunch every day. And he's an observer. He told me yesterday.

He's seen me. But he hasn't told on me.

"Okay," I say. "So you have 'permission.' Tell me more."

He hesitates. He glances down at another sheet of paper on the table. It looks like another list. "I don't want to overwhelm you with information."

"I'm not...overwhelmed."

"...But this has to be a secret."

"I promise," I say. "It's a secret."

"Well, in this interview, Mr. Leland says the labyrinth is a masterpiece. It's geometrically perfect. Do you know how hard that is? To plan and calculate something so that all the angles and curves and turns are perfect?"

I'm not Math Smart, but I bet Will is. He's probably Reading Smart and School Smart, too. He probably knows all the calculations and angles and degrees it takes to make a labyrinth exactly right.

Then I see him looking down at his drawing. He picks up an eraser and goes over a spot where there's still the shadow of a mistake. The labyrinth he has drawn is beautiful to me, but now that we've talked more, I can see him picking apart the imperfections. I know he's seeing that some of the lines are crooked.

"Mr. Leland runs a multibillion-dollar business. He works fourteen hours a day. Seven days a week. He says his doctors have made him try meditation and yoga and everything, but nothing worked. Walking his labyrinth is the only thing that gives him peace. That calms him down."

"That . . . that must be some labyrinth," I say.

Will doesn't speak for a moment and then says, "Yes."

I feel something inside when I hear him talk about this.

"I . . . I really like that," I say.

Will lifts his head up from the article but doesn't look at me. "I know. You said that already."

I sigh. I am the girl who repeats information. I open my lunch. "Anyway, I have rice and chicken. What about you?"

"A cheese sandwich and three bottles of water with one piece of lemon squeezed into each."

I laugh. "Just one? Exactly one in each?"

"Yes. It's the way I like it."

"I get it." I smile to myself and think about my invisible ink. "It's important to be exact when it comes to lemons and water."

I wait for him to launch into a series of little-known

citrus facts, but he doesn't and I look at him and suddenly, I have new information about myself.

I want to feel what it's like to follow a sure and certain path, where there are no choices or dead ends. I want to ask Will if I can come along, but I don't know what he'll say. It feels like such an important mission to him that I think I'm going to have to do something to really earn it. I have to find a way for him to trust me.

I make up my mind, right then and there, that I'm going to make it happen. I'm going to find a way to earn it.

I'm going to become friends with the boy in the striped shirt.

Chapter 16

The waiting on the path has changed.

I'm not waiting for someone to arrive. I'm waiting for a message. A message that means someone out there might just be waiting for me.

Eyes closed. Hand on heart.

> *what if nothing's there*
> *in this place where I expect*
> *and hope for so much...*

It's okay if there's nothing there.

It is.

I bet most people never even get any secret responses to their invisible haiku. If that one note is the only one I ever get, I will go on with my life. I will go on with my life and will always treasure the memory of it.

Okay, I'm lying.

I really want something to be there. Really, really.

I want another answer.

I reach into the Portal with my stick, trying not to be too rough. It takes several tries before I'm finally rewarded with white paper poking out. Is it still the one I wrote? Left there in the Portal to rot? Or is it an answer from my...friend?

I pull it out and open it.

    Hi. I like that poem.

An answer!

    I like what you say about following
    along. I think it's easier.

Do I know who you are? Is that
important? I like that we have a
secret. And no one else has to know.
Will you leave me another poem? And
will you write it in invisible ink
again? I'm glad you're there.

I read it several times and then press it against my
chest as if to prove it's all real. That there's someone
out there who wrote this and is reaching out to me and
wants it to be our secret. And if they want me to be the
invisible poet, I can do that.

Invisibility has sort of become my thing.

Chapter 17

I sit and think a long time before I try to write my response.

Because... how do you keep someone?

I mean, how do you keep someone and make sure they don't leave? How do you figure out how to be and how to act, so they don't even want to begin to *think* about leaving?

I take a breath. Words should never be wasted or rushed. I want everything I write to be real and true and special. And I also want to make sure that I'm not...too much. I want this person to keep writing back. I want them to stay. I just have to figure out how.

Sometimes when I write, I have to work hard to make things sound right. And other times, it's so easy it feels like the lines just appear in the air from my fingertips. But whichever way they come, I know this for sure: I want them to feel like me.

I think today's haiku should be about being grateful that someone is there. And if they want me to write in invisible ink, maybe I need to let them know how grateful I am that they'll be there with a light.

invisible ink
is only invisible
till you bring your light

When I put my first poem in here, I didn't think there was anyone in the world who would know how, or even want, to make it visible again. It's like you saved me from eternal

114

invisibility. So thank you! Thank you!
Thank you!

From,
Your Friend
P.S. I'm now taking special
requests! Is there anything you want
me to write about?

I blow on the lemon juice so that it dries quickly, then roll and tie the note and tuck it into the Portal. I am so glad to have a place where the things inside me can come out and be in the world. I am so, so glad that there's someone who wants to see them.

It takes everything in me to walk away and let whatever happens happen—when all I want is to stand here and wait for an answer to magically appear.

Chapter 18

"Bea! Hi!" Briggs waves at me the second I step into the *Broadside* office the next Tuesday.

He's wearing that same hat again and it's tilted back, so I can see his whole face. Why does he look so happy to see me? We've only really spoken twice. The day I interrupted him midsentence and asked to go to the bathroom after he was nice enough to memorize my poem. Then the time on the path when I was chasing after S's orange-y red sweater and ran into him right before I found the first answer to my haiku.

I give him a little wave back and try to pull my headphones on, but before I can, he's standing there right in front of me. I hesitate and pull them back down.

"So, Bea...is that for Beatrice?"

"...Beatrix."

"Oh yeah. That's right," he says. "Cool."

I don't know what else to say. All I can think is I'll never walk into this office again without my headphones already in place. I start to pull the headphones back up, but Briggs still doesn't let me just get to work. He keeps talking. I pull them back down.

"I like Bea...." he says. "I mean, your name. I like the name...Bea...and you, too, obviously—okay, shutting up." He laughs at himself and yanks his hat over his face. "So, let me show you where the poetry submissions are, and you can see if there's anything you like, and of course you can show me which ones of yours you'd like to use."

I shake my head.

Briggs pushes his hat back up and his straight brows come together over his ruler nose and make a capital *T*. "You don't want to see the submissions?"

"I don't want my...stuff in the paper."

117

"You—really? But...but you have to!"

I do?

Briggs's face. It's so...earnest. Does it mean that much to him?

"C'mon, Bea. Please? I mean, you know I love the blue balloon one, but there was also the 'Buttery, buttery, buttery toast of a morning' one. So good. Really."

I hear myself answer. "Thanks. My dad says..." Stop talking, why am I talking? "...my poems are...what the inside of my head looks like...." *Ugh*. I squeeze my eyes shut for a second. Then open them.

Briggs smiles the smile I think Mrs. Reegs has been talking about. It lights up his whole face, and he looks fun and happy and almost like he doesn't think I'm a total weirdo. "Ha! I like that! And seriously, after Mrs. Reegs sent all those pictures to me, I was excited to meet you—"

I don't know what my face is doing.

"—and then you turn out to be the one who did that awesome dive at the party—"

"That was—" I go red. "I was—just being—"

"It was seriously standing-ovation-worthy—hey!" He points to my ratty old copy of the *Start Your Own*

118

Secret Club book sticking out of my backpack. "I had that book in third grade! Actually, I think everyone in this school has it. I loved the blanket fort section." Briggs continues happily, "My mom used to get so mad, because that whole year, I kept dragging all the blankets outside and they'd be filled with bugs."

I'm not sure what to say next. I look over to where Will is, but he's drawing and didn't even look up when I walked in.

Briggs is still chatting away. "Anyway, you can use the computer over by Jaime. The password is *B, S, I, D, E*; just scroll down and you'll see the mailbox for all the creative writing and poetry. All paper submissions are in the basket by the old typewriter."

I smile and nod and pull my headphones back over my ears. Mrs. Reegs is right. Briggs is really nice. I just hope this is the last time he brings up that dive. I move to the computer. Tami McGee and Anaya wave, but Jaime is busy grooving out to whatever she's listening to. Her head pops up when she notices me. She pulls her headphones down.

"Hey! Briggs told me you were the one who did all those beautiful painting poems?"

I nod and pull my headphones back down. No wonder Briggs and Jaime are friends. So much talking.

"He showed them all to me, like, right after he got them."

Briggs is suddenly standing there.

Jaime turns to him. "Remember? You put them up all over the walls in your room?" She looks back at me. "They looked amazing."

Briggs's mouth drops open. "It's—it's just easier to see submissions that way."

"Is that why they're still up?" Jaime laughs. She turns back to me. "Anyway, I like that you had ink mixed in there, too. I mostly use ink and brush for the comic." She holds out a sketchpad. "See? This is Trini. Her dream is to start a band, but she needs bandmates and a serious band name, and every band needs an epic signature song. So each comic, I get to draw who she meets and think of funny band names and stuff."

"Oh, she's so cute." I can't help smiling. Trini is this chubby turtle in headphones. I kind of want to tell Jaime about my dad and his comic, but I don't want to sound like I'm bragging. Also, was she kidding about Briggs putting my poems on his walls?

"You're so obsessed," Briggs is saying to Jaime. "Just start the band. You've been talking about it and drawing it forever...."

I pull my headphones back on and start reading the submissions in the mailbox while Briggs and Jaime have a marathon talk. I wonder if an epic signature song is sort of like...a theme song.

Every once in a while, I peek over at Jaime. At one point, she softly sings the title of this book I loved when I was little. About an elephant who hears something no one else can. This whole entire world that no one else can even imagine is there. They keep yelling "We're here! We're here!" but no one hears them.

I wonder what song that is. I think I'd like to hear the rest of it someday.

Chapter 19

When I come back to the *Broadside* office for lunch, it doesn't seem like Will is surprised. I think he was expecting me. Not that he says anything or even looks up when I walk in. He just glances at his watch and nods.

I wonder if he has any new Leland information. I start to unpack my lunch.

"You listen to music all the time."

I look up and pull my headphones down. I'm a little

surprised when I hear myself telling him the truth. "Oh. I'm not really listening to anything."

"Then why do you have headphones on?"

I tuck the end of the cord more securely into my pocket. "Just...a habit, I guess."

"A habit means it's something you do all the time. So you must have a reason. A habit by itself isn't a reason."

I pull them off and study Will. I've learned that I have to come up with a satisfying answer or he'll just keep asking me.

"It's a habit because I used to listen to songs all the time. I love how they're a lot like poems. Like, they can be messages that make you feel and realize things. And—and so I made this playlist—"

"What kind of playlist?"

"Just a playlist of songs—"

"What kind of songs?"

"Will, I'm going to tell you. Can you just let me talk without interrupting?"

Will lifts his head from the laptop and says, "Yes." And then looks back down.

"Okay, so they were..." I feel an unexpected sting

in my eyes as I say the next words. "They were like...
theme songs."

"What do you mean, theme songs?"

I can't answer.

"What do you mean, *theme songs*?"

Chapter 20

EVERYONE needs a theme song," S's mom
announced. "They're like little messages to remind
us who we are inside, so we don't forget when we're out
in the world."

S's mom got all her advice from old TV shows.
Whenever she'd disappear for a week or two in her
room, we knew she was power-watching back-to-back
episodes of some series she'd heard about. Last spring,
one of the shows she got obsessed with had a lawyer
who was always pouting and wanting to be in love.

Anyway, someone told this lawyer that all she needed was a theme song to hear in her head to make things better. And as soon as she got one, she started walking around with this bounce in her step, and it was like the world was dancing around her.

So S's mom decided she wanted a theme song, too.

She had been trying to find the right one, but nothing was exactly right. So I offered to help. I did searches online for the Happiest Songs Ever, Best Dance Songs of All Time, and even If You Could Only Hear One Song for the Rest of Your Life, and came up with this huge list for her to listen to. I couldn't believe how many songs were out there that I'd never even heard of before. It could only mean there were tons of other incredible things out there, too, just waiting to be discovered.

S and I spent weeks sitting on the white leather sofa in her living room and watching her mom walk to different songs, waiting for one to put a bounce in her step. I loved those afternoons. She would make us these giant bowls of popcorn with olive oil and flaky salt and just a little bit of cayenne pepper, and we'd hold up these signs I made from poster board with YES! in big bright colors or NO in sad droopy letters.

Then I had this idea that S and I shouldn't hear the songs. We should just watch her walk, and that way we could see which song really made a difference. So S's mom wore my headphones and listened to the songs and walked for us. One song made her sway her hips in this way that made us laugh like crazy and made S scream, "Mom! Stop!" And then another made her jump up and down and dance like a maniac, and then we jumped up and down, too, even though we couldn't even hear the music.

And then something happened.

She started the next song. But she didn't move. She just stood still and listened. And then when she looked at us, her eyes were all filled with tears and her mouth went crooked and she walked straight over and grabbed us and hugged us and we spilled all our popcorn and our signs got all bent, but she didn't care. She whipped the headphone jack out and the song came pouring into the room as she sang the chorus off-key with her arms spread wide open.

It was a really good song. I liked how it made you feel like a book—and that the parts of your life you hadn't figured out yet? Well, they were just waiting to be written. And you got to be the writer. When the song was done, she looked at us and we knew. She had found her theme song.

So I thought S and I should do it, too.

We were walking down the sidewalk when I first heard mine. I had my headphones on, listening to a random shuffle of the list of songs I had—and I knew the second it started. I began walking differently, just like the lawyer from that TV show. Then I was dancing and singing and laughing. But S looked around and grabbed me like I was crazy and made me stop. Which was pretty funny since this was a song all about not letting anyone stop you. But she was so embarrassed and actually looked kind of mad at me.

I tried to get her to listen to some songs I thought would make her want to dance and have fun with me, but she never liked any of the ones I picked.

I stopped looking. I wasn't really worried; I figured it was no big deal. She didn't want to sing and dance on the sidewalk. Fine. I didn't want to do some of the things she was getting into. Like talking about boys. And worrying about stuff like makeup. But lots of people who are best friends have different interests. It doesn't have to mean anything is going to change.

At least that's what I thought when I left for Taiwan.

When I made the playlist for S, I knew it needed a really important name that would explain why I was making it for her. Why I was sending her all these messages. I thought about it for a long time and finally decided to call it *I Hope You Listen*. I drew a beautiful label for her, and I took a picture of it and made it the image that comes up on my phone when the music plays. One of my favorite songs on it is about how it's okay if you're in the middle of a difficult situation. Things will get better. It just takes time.

The only thing is that it's taking a lot more time than I thought it would.

"What do you mean, *theme songs*?"

I look up at Will.

How do I explain this to him?

Will likes the calm turns of a labyrinth, and this story is filled with wrong choices and dead ends. Does it even belong in here in the Zen center of the school?

"They were just songs I collected. Like messages I wanted to send."

"Who do you want to send the messages to?"

I don't answer at first, because I'm not sure I want to share this with him. I like that Will doesn't know everything going on with me.

"I guess I haven't decided yet," I finally say.

He takes this in. Then nods.

"You should decide," he says. "Messages need to be heard."

Chapter 21

At the end of the week, Dad comes home from his latest tour.

He had to fly out to the West Coast to appear at a comic book convention. He sent us a picture of the lines to hear him talk about his latest book, and they wrapped around the entire building. He actually first got noticed because we have the same last name as the guy who created Spider-Man: Lee. But Dad is Steve Lee. Mom says it's part of the reason she fell in love with him. Because Eve will always be a part of Steve. Blech.

When I get home, I run straight into the studio and straight into his arms.

"There's my girl!" he says, and he swings me around and hugs me tight. "Hey, Trix, how's it going? How's school?"

"It's whatever," I say. "Who cares? Tell me, tell me, tell me about the movie. Are they really going to make it?" I can't stop dancing around my dad and hugging him. I hold on to his dumb old sweatshirt from art school that he refuses to throw away. I grab his hands, which always have ink on them.

"Well, we'll see," he says, but he's smiling wide and I know it's going to happen. He's never braggy, no matter what. That's just the way he is. "And how are the girls? I haven't seen them around."

I don't see this question coming and I cough twice so that my mouth can be doing something while I look around for words. Luckily, Mom squeezes between us at that moment to get in on the hugging. I wrap myself around both of them the best I can even though my arms aren't long enough. I wish we could stay like this all afternoon.

"Trix, I want to talk to Daddy about something. Will you go make yourself a snack and do your homework?" Mom smooches him on the cheek.

"But—" I try to hold on to Dad's sweatshirt, even though I can already feel him pulling away. "But it's Friday."

"Is it?" Mom looks at me.

I nod.

She turns back to Dad with her dreamy eyes and dimples. "May I have this dance?"

And she pulls him away toward her magic blue paints and leaves me standing there.

"I love you too much, Trix," he calls out. His voice echoes like it's already a hundred miles away. He doesn't look back. Why would he? If I were pulled into that magic blue dance, I wouldn't, either.

Chapter 22

```
Hi.

    For my special request, I have an
idea: Do you think people are just
the way they are? Or that they can
change if something important is at
stake? Maybe you can write a poem
about that.
```

I lean against the Wall and think of the time S told me to act like I wasn't afraid of Dan Ross's dog. But just because you act a certain way, that doesn't mean it becomes true or real.

Does it?

I mean, what if I just started acting differently? What if... I acted that way I *wish* I were?

> *if I act the way*
> *I wish I were*
> *am I still acting... or becoming?*

Five, four, nine.

Start over.

I watch the lemon juice and water shine and then fade. It doesn't fit in the haiku structure. But I like it. And I don't know how else to explain how I feel. I decide to write it out again.

> *if I act the way I wish I were*
> *am I still acting... or becoming?*

Shine, fade.

I write the lines out over and over again on separate pieces of paper. I want to stay with these words. I want to know them and feel them and watch them sink into the paper where they can stay forever, even if no one else ever sees them. I'm using up all my tiny pages, but it doesn't matter. I can make more.

> *if I act*
> *the way*
> *I wish I were*
> *am I still acting*
> *—or becoming?*

Shine, fade.

Not a haiku. But I like it. I really like it this way. I think my friend will like it, too. I mean, people who are your friends are supposed to like things that are *you*, aren't they?

I roll the piece of paper into a tight cylinder and tie it up with a blade of grass. Then I tuck and tuck and tuck it into the Portal with the tip of my finger and then with the edge of my fingernail and then with a stick until no one can see the poem that's waiting to be seen.

Chapter 23

The next time I see Mrs. Reegs, in the hall between classes, she holds open the door to the Hub and says, "Got a minute?"

"Hi, Mrs. Reegs...sure." I pull down my headphones and go in.

"How's the book?"

Is that what she wants to talk to me about? "Oh. It's so, so good."

"I'm glad. What do you like about it?"

"Well, I...I like the main character and how she's so

fun and different and everyone really likes her." Then I frown. "Except for a couple of people who are kind of mean, but they're really popular...so she should probably do something before they...you know, cause a problem."

"Hmm. That's interesting," Mrs. Reegs says. "What should she do?"

"...I don't think she knows."

"I see," she says. Her voice goes softer. "And what's the worst thing they could do?"

"They could...they could...convince the people who like her not to like her anymore." I feel my eyes sting a little. Because that would be a really sad thing to happen. In this book. "They could take away her people—her Person."

"That would be hard."

I nod.

Mrs. Reegs bends down and carefully reties the silver laces of her sky-blue sneakers. "By the way, Briggs says the deadline for the first quarterly went by and you didn't put any of your own poetry in."

"But I picked out some poems other people did. Didn't you like them?"

She double-knots and looks up. "I loved what you picked. But we were all so excited about the painted poems you were doing. The ones you sent in. Everyone really loved them."

"I loved them, too." My voice comes out smaller and more echo-y than I expect. So I add, "It's just that I'm—I'm done with those. I'm doing something new now."

"Something new? Well, that sounds exciting. I'd love to hear about it."

"Oh. Well, it's...um..." I scan the room and my eyes land on a blank wall. "Invisible ink."

Mrs. Reegs pauses. "Invisible ink for the *Broadside*?"

"Haah!" I try to laugh. "Well, not for the online paper, but I thought we could do it for the printed paper. Like a special edition or something."

"Oh...How would that work, exactly?"

"Well, we could treat the paper with a special invisible ink formula, and then no one would be able to see what's there—until they light a match and hold it underneath and then the heat would slowly make the acid in the ink turn brown...." I look up. "I guess it's a lot of trouble to go through. Especially, if you don't even know if anyone...even wants to see...."

Mrs. Reegs is just watching me. Her Look says she doesn't know what to say.

"It's a terrible idea," I say. "I shouldn't have said anything."

"It's not terrible, Bea. It's just an idea. Ideas mean you're thinking, and that's always good."

"Always?" I say.

She smiles. "Well, some ideas are better than others, Bea, but they're all part of your journey. Good or bad, they all help you grow into who you are and what you're going to be." Mrs. Reegs puts a gentle hand on my head. "If you don't share what's inside you, how will other people ever get to see how wonderful you are? Wouldn't you rather put yourself out there and risk it? Especially if it means a chance to connect with the people who really get you?"

"I don't know," I say. It's all so much to think about. I look up at her. "Is that what you do?"

Mrs. Reegs doesn't answer for a second.

Then she says, "I'm working on it."

Chapter 24

The weeks go by. Mr. Clarke has had a walrus, a horseshoe, a handlebar, and a Dali mustache.

In the hallway, I walk not too fast and not too slow. I keep my headphones on and my music off.

My hands are in my pockets, and my mouth is shut.

I don't write in the sky or close my eyes and I stay as far away from Dan Ross as possible.

At a *Broadside* meeting, I hear Jaime talk about how her mom came from Trinidad and became a DJ and has the biggest music collection *ever*. I try to hear what she's listening to in her epic song search. The other day, I think it was about a bunch of trolls having toast, because she just kept singing "Troll..." every few minutes. "Troll..." And then "Jam! Woo-woo!"

My favorite part of the day is lunch with Will. I walk in. I usually say hi first and open up my lunch. Then Will opens his cheese sandwich and three bottles of water with one piece of lemon each. He comes out of the aquarium now and sits with me. We eat and I listen to the latest news he's gathered on Leland Labyrinth.

Maybe today will be the day we discover some game-changing piece of information.

"Hi," I say as I walk in.

Will looks at his watch. "Hi."

"What're you doing?"

"Making lists."

"Did you get more information about the labyrinth?"

"No."

"Then what are you making lists of?"

"Something else."

"I don't believe it," I say. "Will of the stripèd shirts is making a list about something other than Leland Labyrinth?"

Will stares at his list. "Why don't you believe it?"

I laugh. Then I realize how serious he is. "I'm—I'm just kidding, Will."

"Oh." He puts the lists away. "Do you like Briggs back?"

I pull my headphones down.

"What?"

"Do you like Briggs back?"

"What do you mean, *like him back*?" Of course I like Briggs. Everyone likes Briggs.

"I heard him talking. People talk around me because they just assume that I'm not listening. It's like I'm invisible. You never see me, either."

"I see you—wait, when do I not see you? In class?" Is he upset that we don't talk in those classes we have together? He knows I don't talk in any classes. Plus, Will never gets upset. He's always the same. Steady and matter-of-fact.

"I see you on the path sometimes studying the masonry of that old wall there, but you never see me."

"You see me on the path? By my Wall? Why don't you say hi?"

"You're always late and I don't like to wait. But it doesn't matter. I heard Briggs talking with Jaime yesterday."

"So, they talk all the time. Mrs. Reegs said they grew up together. They're like best friends."

"I know. I heard him telling her that he liked you. That he first saw you at a pool party and then you turned out to be the person who wrote the poems on his wall and now he likes you. I don't know what he'll do. Maybe he'll send you a note about it. Written correspondence is the best because then everything's very clear and you don't have to ask questions. The hat he wears every day was his grandfather's. He died last year."

I start coughing.

I'm not sick and I'm not choking. I think my voice just doesn't know what else to do.

"That's...very sad about his grandfather, but even if Briggs likes me—" I don't know how to finish the sentence. "I don't think of him...that way."

S loved talking about boys liking us one day.

"Maybe we'll transform in seventh grade and become all cool and everyone will freak out and be, like, where did those totally hot girls come from?"

Then she said Dan Ross probably likes me and that's

144

why he picks on me all the time. That's just the way boys are. But her mom overheard and she got really mad and ended up lecturing us for a long time. She said that when someone picks on you, the only thing it means is that *they're the kind of person who picks on other people!* If someone really and truly likes you, they're kind and treat you with respect. End of story.

It made sense to me, but why did anyone have to like anyone at all? Why couldn't we just keep hanging out with our friends and not talk about who likes who or transforming or any of that? Why did I have to think about whether I was hot or cool? Why did we even have to be a temperature?

"You're turning red," Will says.

"I'm not and I think you're wrong." I gather my stuff back up. "I have to go."

"You're leaving. You haven't done that in a while. Your parents will be mad."

I look over to the window where Will will see me Going Stealth in about sixty seconds.

"They won't even care," I say. I hug my backpack

close to me. "They totally trust me to make all my own decisions. They treat me like a grown-up. I mean, they're not even home half the time."

Who else gets to say stuff like this? Who else could leave school whenever they want and never get in trouble?

I'm probably the luckiest kid in the whole school.

Before Will can say another word, I turn and go.

Chapter 25

Forget Going Stealth.

I sprint across the soccer field and rush over to the path and head for the Wall, hoping I have a note from someone who's not making me feel confused. Sixth grade was so easy. Why do things have to change? Why couldn't everything just stay the way it was?

I break two sticks digging into the Portal.

And come up with a small rolled-up note.

```
if I act the way
I wish I were
am I still acting
-or becoming?


This is my favorite thing you've
ever written and I say YES. You can
become any way you want if you just
start acting that way.
    I think it's true. I hope you
think it's true, too.
```

No one has ever quoted my poetry before.

Well, besides Briggs, but I don't want to think about him now.

I don't know who this person—this friend—is, but I do know that I wouldn't have been able to get through these past few weeks without them. This one teeny rolled-up message is enough to erase all the weirdness of that conversation with Will.

I smile at the slightly crooked words with their smudgy edges.

And something occurs to me for the first time.

It's typed. This note.

Typed. Not printed from a computer.

I can tell it's one of those old-fashioned typewriters. The kind with a ribbon and ink. The kind you have to roll sheets of paper into. I know this because S's dad had one a long time ago when we were little and her mom always yelled at him to get rid of it. That was before he moved out in second grade. But I still remember it. Every detail. It had its own carrying case with a leather handle. The keys were black and the letters were worn.

There is a very specific reason I can remember so much about it, even though I haven't seen it since I was seven, and it's because I recently saw one exactly like it.

I see it every day, actually.

The antique typewriter Briggs brought in. The one on the little wooden side table by the steel desk in the *Broadside* office.

Chapter 26

If Briggs is the one I have been spilling my heart out to and sending poems to, I think I will have to leave school and the *Broadside* and this town forever.

I take the stick and dig around until the matches pop out and I stick them in the secret side pocket of my backpack. The one I never use. I stuff my tiny papers in there, too, and I zip it up. Tight. I shove the letter into my jeans to bring to my parents' paper shredder when I get home. I grab the little bottle of invisible ink and toss it over my shoulder. I don't care where it lands.

I walk away from the Portal.

I do not plan to look inside it again.

And I'm hit with a sudden sharp missing of S. She's the one who understands about boys. She would have advice. She would know what to do. Or her mom would have some TV show or lecture to help out.

When you get hurt, you're never supposed to pick at the scab because you'll just hurt yourself more. But sometimes you can't stop yourself from testing the edges a little, and then by the time you realize it's too soft and painful in the center, it's too late and you just have to pull hard and fast and get it over with.

I pull.

I wish S were here.

I really miss having a Person.

We always knew we were best friends, but we didn't know about being someone's Person until S's mom told us about it. It was the year she was obsessed with this show about doctors, and whenever S and I were playing together at her house, she'd hug us and say, "You two are each other's Person!"

She told us we were exactly like the best friends on the show who were always there for each other. And anytime they were upset, they'd stop and dance it out together. We especially loved this one song they danced to. I would pretend to be one girl even though she was Korean and not Taiwanese, and S pretended to be the other girl even though she didn't have the same color hair or eyes. We only found out later that it was my character's last time on the show. And it was a good-bye dance.

I had had a Person for so long that I didn't realize what it would be like not to have one anymore. And maybe that's the way life is and I'm supposed to just dive in and find someone else, but that's not how it works. You can't replace your Person any more than you can replace the people you have a book club with...or walk paths with...or find unexpected Walls with. Because even if you try to replace any of those things, it can never ever really be the same.

Ever.

I turn my back on the Wall and the Portal and find myself looking up the path that leads back to the school.

So maybe I won't look for the same. Maybe I need something different. And I think I might already have it. It may not be much, but it's something:

I have someone who feels the same way I do about labyrinths.

And not many people can say that.

Chapter 27

I brought you soy sauce egg boats," I announce to Will. I'm carrying my favorite lunch box, which my cousins and I got in Taiwan. It's a stack of steel containers that snap together, with a little handle on top. You can stack up to four containers. I usually have just one. Today I added a second, so I could bring extra egg boats and rice with sesame sprinkles for Will. I learned this cute way of serving rice from my aunt. I pack the rice into a little bowl and then flip it upside down to form a mini-mountain and then I sprinkle this seaweed sesame mixture on top. How could anyone say no to that? I even brought two pairs of chopsticks wrapped in napkins. Some people have trouble picking up rice with chopsticks, but I know this trick where you use a little piece of folded paper and a rubber band and it's easy. I can show Will if he wants.

He doesn't even look up. "I don't eat eggs."

"Will. C'mon. Try them. Please? You'll love them. Aren't you sick of cheese sandwiches and lemon water? Don't you like anything else?"

He thinks. "I like hot chocolate. No marshmallows. Just plain. The brand with the cartoon cow."

"Okay. That's something. So why not add these delectable soy sauce eggs to your menu?" I wave my hands over my lunch box.

"I don't eat eggs."

"Well, you've never tried soy sauce eggs cut into little boats. My mom used to make these for me when I was little."

"Did your mom make these? You said she *used* to make them. Past tense. So it sounds like she doesn't make them anymore."

"I—I made them. I always make my own lunch.

My mom's busy with her new show coming up—and I'm very independent. My parents don't treat me like a little kid."

"You said that before. About your parents."

"Seriously, Will. Do you always have to remember everything?"

"I remember everything because I listen. That's why you only have to tell me something once. If you listened better, you wouldn't always need everything repeated. You should listen."

"Okay. Listen to this: I think it wouldn't kill you to change things up a little bit. Like a new lunch. Or have you ever worn anything besides a short-sleeved striped shirt? What do you own, like, twenty of those?"

"These don't have tags in the back, so my mom bought a lot of them. I don't like tags. Or long sleeves."

"It's November, Will. Don't you have a jacket?"

"I don't need one yet. I'm only outside for ten minutes when I walk each way to school and back."

I pause when he mentions the walking. I've been wanting to ask him something. We have two classes together in the afternoon. I sit in the front in both, and he sits in the back corner. We don't talk before or after class. We've sort of limited our ... time together to lunch here in the secret Zen place. So we only really see each other once a day.

"You know ... if you want, we can meet up and walk on the path together ... before and after school."

"No."

Just like that. No. "But ... why not?"

"Your locker is at the opposite end of the building. Mine is on this side."

"So then let's just plan on meeting each day by the middle exit. Listen. From now on, I promise, anytime you want to walk with me, I'll be there five minutes after the last bell."

"No. I don't like waiting. I just want to walk when I walk."

I'm bewildered. "Everyone wants what they want, Will, but if you just wait—"

"I don't like waiting."

"But can't you change for a frien—for ... other people?"

"Do you change for other people?"

I take the eggs back. "Fine. You don't like eggs. Or waiting. Or change. At least you can say THANK YOU. It's—it's just really, really important. How else

157

is anyone supposed to know that you appreciate them at all?"

"THANK YOU," Will says. "Why would you bring me lunch when you know I bring my own every day?"

I poke at an egg boat with my chopsticks. "I don't know....I had extra. I just...I didn't want to waste. That's all. So, now we can go back to talking about nothing but what *you* want to talk about." I add the last part in a low voice.

Will looks down at his lists and thinks for a moment. "That's a good idea."

I frown. "What is? Talking about nothing but what you want?"

"Not wasting. Not wasting things is a good idea." He traces down his paper with a finger. "You don't like to waste words." Then he writes something on the bottom.

What is he even talking about?

As he picks up a water bottle, his folder falls to the floor and slides toward me.

"I've got it!" I say. "Because I'm a kindly and generous person and I do things for others." I even straighten out the papers and am about to tuck them back in the folder when I see my name.

Beatrix Lee

1) No Leland information

2) Needs things explained several times

3) Likes to repeat things

4) Likes haiku (5, 7, 5) bc doesn't like to
   waste words

5) No music

6) Lunch every day

7) Always on time

And then at the bottom, penciled in:

8) Say THANK YOU to show appreciation

I almost drop it again but recover and quickly hand
it all to Will.

"THANK YOU for picking up my folder and
THANK YOU for bringing me lunch," he says.

I don't answer. Because my mind is going a million
miles an hour and I think I know what the list means.

This list named Beatrix Lee.

Will makes lists of things that are important to him.
Things he needs to practice. Like the Leland estate and

how to break in. He's smart in some ways, but not others. He's Planning Smart. And Observing Smart. But the way he acts sometimes, he isn't always People Smart. And I think this list is about him practicing to be… Friend Smart.

For me.

We sit in silence for a while.

"So, THANK YOU," he says again. "But I still don't want the eggs."

"Okay," I say.

I'm about to start eating, but I can't because my mouth is doing something weird, and it takes me a moment to realize that I'm smiling so hard it hurts.

Chapter 28

I want to do something for Will.

And I know he doesn't like soy sauce egg boats. And it's not as if we'll find theme songs together or dance it out or anything. But I still want to do something. And I know exactly what it is.

I want to find a way to get him into Leland Labyrinth.

One of the first things he ever asked me was if I had any information he could add to his list, so he could figure out a plan to break into the Leland estate. But now

I think I just might have something even better than information.

I have my mom. And her art.

If Mr. Leland loved it enough to buy two of her giant paintings for the lobby of his famous building in the city, maybe he'll give me permission to get onto his property.

I thought I could go to his office and introduce myself and ask Mr. Leland if Will and I could explore the labyrinth while my mom hung out with him or something. People always want to hang out with artists and see what they're like in real life.

Though the last time I went into the city without grown-ups, it didn't exactly turn out great.

There was a grand opening of this new candy store and it was such a big deal, it was in the news. S and I were obsessed with it, but none of our parents would take us. Mine had to work and S's mom had a hair appointment with this new stylist at Salon de Jean René she had waited forever for.

So S decided we should just go on our own. She knew I was City Smart. That I knew my way around all the trains and subways and had been going in with my parents since I was little. She begged and begged until I finally caved in. I mean, they were giving away free sugar tattoos that you could lick off. We had to be there. So we told our parents we were biking up around the Neck that whole Saturday, and since there's never any cell service there, we knew they wouldn't call us to check up on our whereabouts.

My memory of that day will always be like a movie montage of dancing and shouting and candy-eating scenes, set to the song they blasted as the doors opened for the first time.

Towers of every color jelly beans!

Rock candy like giant pastel jewels!

Sparkly sour gummies, shimmering under their sugar coating!

Toffees! Taffy! Chocolates!

We had worn matching shirts tied at the waist and swirly skirts, and we hadn't eaten anything all day, so we'd have more room for candy. There were three floors and the stairs were clear blocks of glass that looked like ice with candy frozen inside them. We couldn't stop grabbing free samples and buying everything our allowances could afford.

When we missed our train home, because we were

too busy throwing up in Penn Station, we had to call our parents, crying. It was one of the few times I ever got in trouble. My dad asked why I would sneak off and do something that was So Not Me—even if it was for a friend. I didn't know how to tell him that S was worried that L and L weren't hanging out with us as much and that she just needed to know I would do anything for her.

This time will be different. No one needs to talk me into it. It's my idea.

I peek into the studio. "Mom, I need a mental health day today. Can you sign a note for me to bring to school on Monday?"

Mom doesn't even look up as she waves a smudgy blue hand. "Mmm-hmmm!"

And just like that, I have permission. Well, sort of like how Will has permission from Mr. Leland's niece to walk the labyrinth. I'm recognizing my mom's permission for a mental health day. I'm not sneaking off. I'm just not being specific about where I'm going.

There's a little basket on this table by the front door filled with ten-trip passes for the train and MetroCards for the subway, because Mom can never keep track of how many she's bought. I grab one of each and tuck them into a cute little bag I borrowed from her closet. The train station's an easy walk and I set off with plenty of time.

I am so pleased with myself and so happy to be doing this for Will that it isn't until I board the train that I begin to wonder:

What kind of security do they have there?

Do I need some kind of pass to get in?

What if the guards have Killer Hounds in matching uniforms?

I may be City Smart, but I'm definitely not Planning Smart. I wanted to surprise Will, but I probably should've asked him to help me make a list of the information I needed before I decided to just walk into one of the most famous buildings in the city and ask an eccentric billionaire to put away his Killer Hounds and give me and my friend permission to walk his labyrinth.

Chapter 29

I've known the Leland & Leland Building my whole life. We pass it whenever we go to the gallery that shows my mom's art. And, of course, we went there to visit the paintings Mr. Leland bought when they were first hung in the lobby.

I've been inside the lobby exactly two times. Both with my parents. My mom had to oversee the delivery of her pieces, and she let me cut school that day to come along. And then we were there for the official unveiling of her art, which was like a party they had right in the lobby with all these fancy appetizers and drinks and everything.

From the outside, the building is all black marble and the windows are tinted, so it almost looks like it doesn't have any windows at all. My dad calls it the Monolith, and every time we've been here, he's stood out front singing, "...dummm...duuuMMMM... duuUUUMMMMMM—DAH-DUUMMMMMMM!"

And then he jumps around and pretends to be a screaming monkey, and Mom and I laugh like crazy. Mom said it's from this weird movie and that watching Dad's bit is better than the whole thing.

When I get there, I stand outside for a minute and hum Dad's Monolith song to myself. I don't do the full monkey screams like he does, though I'm pretty sure no one in the city would really notice. A cowboy with no pants just walked by and not a single person turned their head.

Inside, it looks like I've just walked onto the set of a science fiction movie called *The Future*. The walls and floors are all shiny, blinding white. There are no dark corners or cozy nooks to hide in. It's all cold stone and glass doors.

The only color comes from my mom's art. And me.

And now I'm worried that I'm wearing the wrong thing. Everyone else is in black or gray or navy, and I'm wearing my mom's long paint-splattered skirt with a pink-and-orange 1970s dress shirt of my dad's that she likes to wear tied at the waist. My hair is knotted on top of my head with a paintbrush stuck through it, just like I've seen her do. Though it took me three tries to get it to stay and now it sort of hurts my head.

People keep pouring through the automatic doors. I step to the side and look around. Instead of a front desk, there's a huge slab of white marble the size of a ship. You can't pass it unless you wave a card at the glass gates on the left or right side. A man in uniform stands at each end. But at least there's no sign of Killer Hounds.

I study the two guards. S and I saw a movie once where this guy has to choose which cup to drink out of. If he chooses poorly, he turns a thousand years old in, like, ten seconds. If he chooses wisely, he lives forever. Decisions can be life changing.

Both guards are scowling, but the one on the right just a little bit less. I choose him. My heart is pounding as I walk over.

"Hello, how are you? I'm Beatrix Lee, daughter of Eve Lee, the artist. I've come to see Mr. Leland...."

His scowl deepens and deepens until it is way worse than the other guard's. My heart sinks. I have chosen poorly.

"...Please?" I squeak.

"Artist?" His voice is deeper than any voice I've ever heard before. He points to one of my mom's giant paintings. "Like, that artist?"

I nod. Grateful Mr. Leland bought my mom's art before her naked blue stage.

The scowl shifts into a smile. "You don't say. I met her once. That's your mom? She is one cool lady."

I have chosen wisely!

"So, do you have an appointment, daughter of the artist?"

I take a big breath. "You know, I didn't even have time to call. I just need to speak with him about...a personal matter." And I smile again. The way my mom does. Like I'm completely sure that everyone's here to make my life even lovelier than it already is.

Maybe I am my mother's daughter, because it works. "Well, all right then, Beatrix Lee, artist's daughter. Nice to meet you. You can call me Brandon." He points to a name tag that says C. BRANDON. We shake hands. His is the size of a frying pan.

I pull out a small stack of photos that Dad took of Mom and me the day of the unveiling, standing in front of her pieces titled *This No. 1* and *This No. 2.*

The last photo is Mr. Leland, Mom, and me. It almost looks like he's smiling with his mouth open, but I remember that he was actually in the middle of shouting "Haven't you taken it yet?" when the flash went off.

"Will you look at that," says Brandon.

"I'm so excited to see, uh, *Mr. L* again. He totally said I could just stop by whenever I was around."

Brandon looks at me and lowers his voice. "Listen, I'm not supposed to let you up without an appointment, but I like you. You look like the kind of person who will shake things up. Am I wrong?"

I shake my head. Then I think, Wait, am I shaking my head *No, you're wrong* or *No, you're right*?

"You know, you're lucky you came over to this side, Beatrix Lee. Two kinds of people in this world: the Brandons"—he points to himself—"and the Grubers." He jerks his head toward the guard at the other end, who's angrily talking through his teeth to a delivery person.

He glances around, then picks up a card from behind the marble ship and waves it in front of the glass gate. As it opens, he points me toward a bank of elevators around the corner. "Tell *Mr. L* Brandon says hi!" He chuckles and waves.

"I will, I promise!" I say, and I rush over to the elevators and jump into the closest one before he has a chance to change his mind.

Yes! I did it! I'm in!

Ding!

The elevator door closes and I look at all the buttons.

There are forty-four floors in this building.

And I have no idea which one *Mr. L* is on.

Chapter 30

I just stand there wondering what to do. After a few minutes, when I don't push any buttons, the doors ding and open again.

A man in a stiff suit is standing there. He frowns at me and steps to the side to let me off. He thinks I just came down the elevator. I don't know what to do or say, so I just stare at the ceiling. Finally, he sighs a huge sigh and comes in and punches the button for the fourteenth floor. Then glares at me. For a second, I wonder if I can get some information from him about where to find Mr. Leland, but I decide against it. He's definitely a Gruber.

I pick twenty-five and push that. He'll get off first, then I can find a bathroom on my floor and hide until I figure out what to do next. I keep staring at the numbers. My heart is hammering and I'm feeling faint.

When we finally get to fourteen, the man storms off, muttering, "Place of business, not a playground!"

The doors close behind him and I look at the dull reflection staring back at me.

What was I thinking? Look at me. I'm nothing like my mom, even if I have this dumb brush stuck in my hair. And the paint-splattered skirt, which looks so cool on her, just makes me look like a messy kid. If I don't leave now, I'll end up causing a scene. I begin to hit random buttons. I have to make a run for it. I have to get out of here.

Ding!

The elevator stops and I launch myself at the door as it opens—and almost crash into a woman in a dark suit with crazy pink high-heeled shoes. She's trying to hold the door open for a tall man with a headful of hard silvery hair.

It's him.

It's Mr. Leland.

I stare up at him with my mouth open. I forgot how tall he is. His hair looks like he sprayed it with shellac and even a tornado would not budge it.

I'm in the elevator with Mr. Leland. Tall, shellac-head Mr. Leland.

"Oh, I'm sorry, are you getting off?" the woman says.

Mr. Leland frowns down at me in my messy skirt. The paintbrush slipping out of my hair. I should never have come. I have chosen poorly.

I push past them and run out.

Chapter 31

*D*ing!

"Bea?"

Ding! Ding! Ding!

I turn.

The woman in the pink heels is holding the door.

"It is Bea, isn't it?" *Ding!* "We met when your mother hung her art—" *Ding!* She looks at me and laughs. "Why don't you come back in, so this elevator can stop having a temper tantrum?"

I pause. It's my chance. Do I stay or go? Choose!

I step back into the elevator, and the doors finally close.

"Sorry," I say.

"For what? It's so nice to see you. What are you doing here?" The woman smiles at me.

"I…" I glance up at Mr. Leland.

"Do I know you? What do you want?" His voice is cold and tight.

I open my mouth and nothing comes out.

The woman shakes her head at him and holds a hand out to me. "I'm Jenny Leland. We met at the party for your mom's art."

I take her hand and then I realize I'm giving her what my dad calls the dead fish handshake, so I try to make it firmer, but I squeeze too hard and she gives a little jump.

"Oh!"

"Sorry—"

Jenny Leland laughs and rubs her hand. "No, I like a good handshake."

I'd like to disappear right now.

"So, Beatrix, no school today?"

"Oh. Um, no. No school because…parent-teacher

176

conferences! That's it. All day. So…no classes." I peek over at Mr. Leland. "I'm going to meet my mom at her gallery, but I thought I'd stop here and look at her art in the lobby first."

But he is not the least bit interested in why I'm here. He didn't even turn when I mentioned my mom. His arms are crossed and his chin up, eyes glued to the elevator numbers.

The elevator dings again and we're on his floor. He marches out without looking back, but Jenny catches the door and beckons me through. She nods toward the reception area.

"I'll be back," she mouths.

I sit down and try to make myself comfortable, but the steely gray sofas don't give at all. I glance at a stack of magazines on the side table next to a strange potted plant, but they're arranged *just so* and I wouldn't dream of taking one.

After ten minutes, she comes back out and smiles. "I'm so sorry. My uncle is in one of his moods, as you clearly saw, and I had to update him on an account that's a real mess."

"Did that make it worse?" I ask. How am I ever

going to ask him for a favor? He's already in such a bad mood.

Jenny Leland laughs. "Actually, better. Problem-solving always helps him relax."

"Really?" I ask.

"Nothing in the world calms him down more."

I smile to myself. I can think of something. And it's the very reason I'm here.

"So Mr. Leland is your uncle?"

"Yes. I'm one of the creative directors here, and I'm proud to say, I'm the one who chose your mom's paintings for our lobby."

Oh. I thought Mr. Leland chose them.

"You?"

She nods. "I've been a fan of your mom's work for-ever. You just can't help feeling connected to it; it's perfect. When my uncle let me take the lead on the art purchase, I knew I was going to buy from her. Any-way, would you like to come into my office and talk a little?"

I nod.

She's so nice and so pretty with her bouncing dark bob of hair and her high, high heels. And she loves my mom. She leads me around the corner and down the hall. Her office has a glass door that's half-frosted, so from the outside you can see she's there without really seeing everything that's going on inside. It reminds me of Will's aquarium corner at the *Broadside*.

We sit on these nice soft pink sofas and she says, "So, Beatrix, what can we do for you?"

I take a deep breath. "I have a friend...."

"You have a friend."

"And he wrote to you. He...he has this thing for..." I look up at her. "He loves...labyrinths."

She snaps her fingers. "Will. Of course, I remember him." But then she sighs. "I'm sorry, Bea. I know what this is about. Will caught me in an optimistic moment. I'd just won a huge account and was feeling unstoppable. Have you ever felt that way?"

I shake my head. Unstoppable. I can't even imagine that.

"I told him I was sure I could get him in—which was a mistake, because my uncle just refused. He's a smart businessman, but *nooooot* so good with people, as you saw earlier."

I can't help smiling a little. Jenny Leland and I have

something in common. We both know what it's like to be around someone who's Really Smart, but not always People Smart.

"Have you ever been inside?" I ask. It must be the Zen-est of all Zen places if walking that path can make Mr. Leland even a tiny bit calm.

"With my mom when I was little, but it was never really my thing. Even back then Uncle Henry was always so protective of it. Though lately, he's been threatening to tear it down."

"Tear it down?" What would Will think? "But I thought it was his masterpiece."

"Believe me, it's the most beautiful thing you've ever seen. But still not good enough. He wants to yank out all the hedges and rebuild it in ancient stone, so it's more authentic."

"Wait. Ancient stone?" I slam my hand down on her table. "You mean stonework. That's—that's masonry! Will knows everything about masonry." Well, that might be an exaggeration, but it was one of the first things Will ever mentioned to me. And Mr. Leland's thinking that his masterpiece labyrinth still isn't good enough reminds me so much of Will and his drawings.

"They have to meet! I mean, wouldn't your uncle like that? I actually think they're a lot alike, and I'll bet Will has great advice to give him. He could help!"

Jenny shakes her head. "I'm sure Will is a very bright boy, Bea, but trust me, I know my uncle when it comes to things like this. It's not even worth trying—the wall around the estate just got damaged and he won't even *discuss* it with anyone except the family of the original masons who built it back in the sixties. He drove his assistant crazy when he found out they weren't in New York anymore."

"They moved?" I ask, though I don't really care. The whole thing is starting to feel hopeless, and I just want to keep Jenny talking until I find a way to convince her to help me.

"To the Windy City." She looks at my blank face. "Chicago."

Oh. I like the way that sounds. *The Windy City.* "So I guess he'll have to find another mason—hey! Will could help him! He's great at finding information—"

Jenny shakes her head again, more firmly. "He only wants the original family to do the repair. So he's going to fly them out here." She leans toward me. "On. His.

Private. Jet. I'm really sorry, Bea, but unless Will has a PhD in ancient stone and comes from a long line of Greek masons, he's of no interest to my uncle."

I jump up. "I just remembered. I have to go...."

Jenny stands, too. "Oh! Well, I understand. I have things to do, too. But I hope you come back. I really do love your mom's work and I'd love to have both of you come visit or take a tour of the building. Can I show you out?"

I shake my head. "No, I remember the way. Thank you, Jenny. I'll—I'll let my mom know how nice you were. And ask if she wants to come one day."

"That would be great. Maybe we can have lunch. Call me anytime."

She hands me a business card.

I take it and nod and try to put a big smile on my face, but all I can think is that I have to get out of here.

Fast.

Fast, but not too fast.

Because if you go too fast, people get suspicious.

They know something's up. And something is definitely up.

Will taught me to pay attention to details while

gathering information, and Jenny Leland just said that her uncle *is going* to fly the masons here to fix the big wall that surrounds the Leland estate. Is Going. Future tense. As in, it hasn't happened yet.

Will also told me that everyone has a vulnerable spot. A weakness.

It looks like the Leland estate has one, too.

We just have to get to it before the Windy City masons.

Chapter 32

"I got it!" I say as I burst into the *Broadside* office on Monday.

I blink. All the lights are off. And Will's not here.

He's always the first one here.

Where could he be? Why isn't he sitting in his aquarium, checking his watch as I walk in? Should I wait?

I sit at the table where I'm usually already unpacking my lunch and getting ready to tease him about his daily cheese sandwich. I'm thinking about leaving when the door finally opens and Will comes in. Followed by

Mrs. Reegs. She flips half the light switches the way she always does, and the lamps around the room go on, filling it with the warm Zen glow that only happens here.

I jump up. "Oh. Mrs. Reegs. Hi. I know I'm not supposed to be in here." I hold up my lunch box. "I meant to ask you for permission—"

"It's fine." Mrs. Reegs is smiling wider than usual. But it doesn't look like a real smile. It's too tight. "Will tells me you've been having lunch with him every day. I'm so glad."

Will doesn't look at me. He walks straight over to the steel desk. He has his folder with him. He's bending and unbending the corner. He doesn't unpack his lunch. He sits and then stands and then sits again. He keeps looking at his watch.

Mrs. Reegs glances at him, then me. I can't read her Look. "We just had a small change in schedule last period—"

"It's not a small change when someone doesn't show up," Will says. His voice is a little bit louder than usual. "I told her the schedule. She knew."

"Who?" I ask. "Who knew?"

"My mom," Will says.

"Why did your mom have to come here?" Was Will

185

in trouble? Did someone find his lists about breaking into the labyrinth? What if Jenny Leland figured it all out and called the school?

"I don't want to talk about it. She was a no-show and that's that."

"She left a message, Will," Mrs. Reegs says. Her voice sounds low. And private. Maybe I should go. "It was just a mix-up at the front desk."

Will begins to push at his temples. "I don't want to talk about it, Fee. Just stop." He doesn't look up. "You weren't here on Friday."

It takes me a second to realize he's talking to me. "Oh. I'm—I had something important to do." Is he upset I wasn't here? Or upset with Mrs. Reegs? I've never heard anyone speak to her like that. Everyone loves her.

"My mom doesn't show up for stuff sometimes," I offer.

Mrs. Reegs looks at me and nods. "It's just something that happens with parents, isn't it?"

"Definitely," I say. I'm glad I can help. "I mean, with her big show coming and my dad on tour, sometimes I don't see them for days. Not for dinner or breakfast or anything..."

Mrs. Reegs looks startled. "Really?"

Before I can answer, the door swings open and Briggs comes in. "There you are, Mrs. Reegs. The high school editor was asking if you knew where—" He sees me and smiles his whole-face smile. "Hey, Bea!" He sees Will and waves. "Hi, Will."

I look at Will, who knows that Briggs likes me, and I look at the typewriter and then I look at Mrs. Reegs. I don't know what to say.

Then the door flies open again and two tall boys come in. High school seniors, I bet. They look like they probably shave and have hairy armpits and buy the kind of deodorant that says stuff like *Now in Extra Strength*.

"What up, Reegster?" one of the boys says. "Why's it so dark in here?" He swipes under the DO NOT CHANGE LIGHTS sign.

And everything changes.

One by one, the ceiling lights power on, buzzing and flickering to full force. I look up and blink against the glare, then see spots. The Zen is gone.

The other boy has gone over by Will.

"Can I get in? I think I left my flash drive in here—" He tries to slide a drawer open in the space between Will and the front of the steel desk.

187

Will is squinting. He shakes his head no.

But the boy doesn't notice and starts rustling around inside. Will's folder flies off the top and papers swoosh in different directions onto the floor.

"Travis," says Mrs. Reegs. "I need to talk to you, right away—"

"Sure, Reegs. Give me a—"

"Stop." Will shakes his head again. "You're messing up my—"

"Chill, kid—"

"Stop—"

Briggs gets to Will's corner so fast, it's almost like he's been standing there the whole time. "I told you guys I'd come in and get it for you." He doesn't seem to care that this boy is way older. And bigger. "Give him space."

Something is wrong, but I don't know what. And it's not just the lights. Something feels...off.

I look back at Will.

He's shaking his head harder and harder and harder. Then he presses his hands over his ears and—just like that—sinks to the floor. He won't stop shaking his head or squeezing his ears like he wants to tear his head off.

What's happening?

I look from Will to Mrs. Reegs. I don't know what to do.

Mrs. Reegs's voice is careful. "Let's clear the room, everyone. Everything's fine."

But everything's not fine.

"C'mon, guys," Briggs says.

The high school boys look at each other but finally begin to file out.

I gather the papers that have flown out of Will's folder. He would hate that. He would hate his papers all over the place.

"Let's give Will a minute," Mrs. Reegs says. "I'll walk you both out. He's got this."

She leans in and says something to Will, but I can't hear what it is. It doesn't look to me like he's stopping anytime soon, and I don't think he's got this. When Mrs. Reegs gets to the door, she turns off the overhead lights.

I follow her, hugging Will's folder to my chest. The folder with a list inside that has my name on it.

Mrs. Reegs opens the door. Her voice is low. "Briggs, do you mind mentioning to everyone out there that he'll be okay and ask them not to make a big deal out of it?"

Briggs nods, then glances at me and leaves.

"They'd better not make a big deal out of it," I say. "Will can't help it if—if…" I don't know how to finish the sentence.

Mrs. Reegs looks at me a moment. Then continues in that same low voice. "It's…hard for Will sometimes when too many things change unexpectedly…when things he's counting on are taken away…it—it just becomes too much."

Days that are too much.

I know what that's like. I glance back at Will. *Jenga*.

"This is where he usually comes to get away during school. It's like a safe place for him, but, well, now…"

"Tell me what to do," I say. "I can be his Person. I can help him feel safe."

"Oh, Bea," Mrs. Reegs says. "That's so—" She stops. "I—I'm sorry, Bea, but I shouldn't have said anything. Will's mom—" She stops again. And takes a breath. "Thank you for wanting to help, Bea. And especially for being a friend to Will. Everything will be okay. I promise. You should go on to lunch." She's still holding the door open. But I don't move. She watches me for a minute with her forehead all crinkled up, then asks in a soft voice, "How's the book?"

I look down at her sneakers. Today, gray with darker gray stripes.

"Bad. Things are going wrong," I say. "I don't know if I want to keep reading...."

Mrs. Reegs nods. "I know. It's hard—when you don't know what's going to happen." She reaches a hand out. "I'll bring that back to Will." She takes the folder from me and tucks the papers in securely. "I told him it'd be easier with a spiral notebook—"

"But he doesn't like the little pieces of paper that get stuck when you rip out the pages."

Mrs. Reegs's eyes are soft as she looks at me. "I hope you give the book a chance," she says, and she goes back in and lets the door close.

Briggs is waiting for me down the hall. Jaime is just walking up as I get there.

"Do you want to come have lunch?" he asks, eyeing my lunch box.

Jaime smiles. "Please come!" She yanks down her headphones. "Also, Bea, tell me you play an instrument. I've decided I'm going to do the band. I mean, I have my uke, and Briggs has been rocking the oboe since third grade." She laughs. "All we need is a few more people and—what? What's wrong?"

Briggs looks at me. But I don't know what to say, so I just turn and walk away. He can explain about Will to Jaime if he wants.

Then Jaime calls out, "Bea! Wait up!" and I take off.

I don't want to be there, but I don't know where I want to be. I look down the hall one way and then the other. When I found Will and the *Broadside* office, I thought I was done with not knowing where to go during lunch. I see the back exit. And make a run for it.

Will's mom won't be the only no-show today.

Though I can't really be a no-show if no one is waiting for me anywhere.

Chapter 33

When I get to the clearing by the Wall, I do what I always do here. I let myself take a deep breath and feel the beginning of a calm that only this place can give to me. And I know it's because this place—this is my safe place. Just like the *Broadside* is Will's. How would I feel if my place weren't safe anymore?

I think about what Mrs. Reegs said. About how hard it was for Will when important things changed.

Like his mom being a no-show.

And the high school kids changing the Zen lights and messing up his papers.

And...maybe even me not being there on Friday.

I have to find a way to get Will to Leland Labyrinth. I want to take him to the masterpiece of all Zen safe places. It's not right and it's not fair for Mr. Leland to keep it all to himself.

A twig snaps behind me and I spin around.

Briggs is there with Jaime. Her headphones are down and she's searching my face.

"You looked upset," she says. "We wanted to make sure you're okay."

Briggs is looking around. "We're kind of far off campus. Maybe you should walk back with us before we get in trouble."

I shake my head and cross my arms. "I want to stay out here."

"I'll stay with you," he blurts out. "Just the two of us can talk if you want."

Jaime looks from Briggs to me. Then me to Briggs. And one eyebrow goes way up. She shakes her head, then pulls her headphones back on and leaves.

I wait till she disappears around the corner. "Is she upset?"

Briggs looks down the path. "Yeah ... I'll talk to her. She's mad at me, not you. She just—she wants you to hang with us, but she doesn't know if you like her. I told her you're just ... quiet."

"Oh." How could anyone *not* like her? Or Briggs? "But why didn't you tell her to stay, then?"

"Because—you know she's not my girlfriend, right? She's, like, my best friend. I've known her since we were little. I just didn't want you to think—" Briggs is red again.

"I know that," I say before he can keep going. "Mrs. Reegs told me you grew up together, and I don't think— I wasn't even thinking anything. About that."

Rustling bushes make me think maybe Jaime's back, listening in on this mortifying conversation. I turn, but there's no one there. There never is.

Briggs pushes his hat off his face. "We can talk ... about Will. If you want."

I do want to talk about Will.

I nod.

"Will was a year behind us at Westside," Briggs says. "When he started here this year, Mrs. Reegs asked if he could join the paper and if I would sort of...befriend him. He doesn't really hang out with anyone, but we always got along fine."

Befriend.

It's a good word.

Be...Friend

I like that.

"He used to have those...breakdowns...sometimes, a couple of years ago. Mrs. Reegs has known Will since he was little. So I guess she's always helped him out. I asked what was wrong with him one time, and she said there was nothing wrong with him, he just has a different way of thinking and seeing things. She said everyone does. Even, like, you or me. I don't even remember the last time he—you know—had that happen. Mrs. Reegs says he has some kind of a—a routine or something now that helps him."

I know Will's routines.

He makes lists of information.

He draws conclusions.

And then he practices whatever it is he's figured out.

I think that drawing and walking labyrinths are how he practices calming down, and I want to help him. I think of Briggs befriending Will. Telling the seniors to go. And I make a choice.

"Can I tell you something?" I ask.

"You can tell me anything."

I swallow. "Well. There's this thing going on. It has to do with the Leland estate."

"Up on the Neck? With the Killer Hounds?"

"I don't even want to think about them," I say. "But they're probably going to be a problem, because Will is obsessed with getting on that property and—"

"The maze," Briggs says. "He wants to see the maze, right?"

"Labyrinth—but yes. He wants to see it."

Briggs nods. "He's always drawing them. So, how's he going to do it—get in to see the labyrinth? Old Man Leland never allows visitors. He built that huge wall around the whole property. It's like a fortress."

I take a deep breath and look him in the eyes. "That fortress wall that guards the property?"

He nods.

"I think there's a way in."

There is more rustling in the bushes behind us. But this time, it gets wilder, as if something is off-balance in there. And then someone comes tumbling out onto the path.

It's...S.

I try to meet her eyes, but she won't look up. Then, a few seconds later, voices and footsteps come around the corner with laughing and chatter that I recognize with my heart before the reality of it hits my brain.

L and L and A come bursting into the clearing. "She went this way! What are you—" They stop when they see me. They look at Briggs. Then at S. "What's—"

S jumps up. "I fell. I was running home because I forgot my homework. But I don't even care—"

The girls are staring at me and Briggs. A grabs S by the arm and starts dragging her away. "C'mon, let's go...."

Then they're all gone almost as quickly as they came.

"That was weird," says Briggs. He lowers his voice. "Listen, can you not tell anyone any of the stuff I said about Will? I think his mom doesn't want people talking about it."

I nod. Who would I tell?

Briggs frowns. "But I think that's kind of messed up. I think people should talk about things. How is anyone supposed to understand anything and how are things supposed to get better if you don't talk about it?"

I don't know. I understand not wanting to talk about things. And if it's so important to Briggs to talk, I'm not sure how much more I want to tell him.

"Actually, you know what? Never mind. I think I'm making a bigger deal of it than it actually is. Just forget it," I say, shrugging. "There are lots of mazes Will can go to. He was just talking about them the other day. . . ." My voice trails off and I scratch my nose. It's not even itchy. I just need to do something that covers my face.

We sort of stand there awkwardly for another minute, till Briggs says, "Well, I guess I'd better get back . . . lots to do . . . lunch is almost over. . . ."

"Okay, sorry."

"For what?"

I don't know. "Dragging you out here, I guess."

"You didn't. I wanted to come out."

"Oh."

"You can drag me out here anytime," Briggs says. Then he looks mortified. Then he laughs and pulls his fedora over his eyes and starts heading back to school.

And I suddenly think that my mom would like Briggs very much. Because he wears his heart on his sleeve. Everything he's thinking and feeling is just out there all the time. There's no guessing. And that's the way she is.

Only, my mom doesn't just wear her heart on her sleeve, she wears it on her canvas, too. Like when her art totally changed after we got back from Taiwan and became the naked blue paintings. She said she couldn't help it; she had to show what was inside her.

The heart on the sleeve. I think, maybe, it's something that I like, too.

"Briggs!"

He turns. "Yeah?"

"Oh . . . nothing," I say. I wave.

He waves back and keeps walking.

I watch him go. *Thank you for the notes.*

I look at the empty Portal for a moment.

And I'm sorry I stopped writing to you.

I turn and walk home.

Chapter 34

The next day at lunch, I brace myself before I walk into the *Broadside* office because I'm afraid Will won't be there and I'll be alone again. No. It's not just that. I want to make sure he's okay. I want to see that his safe place is safe again. I want to tell him about my adventure at Leland & Leland. How I observed and paid attention and got the information. I want to plan the break-in with him. I want this to be something we do together.

He's sitting there like it's just another day. Today

with his laptop. I walk over and set my lunch down and then peek to see what he's reading. Leland research. He glances at his watch and I smile.

"Hey…"

"Hi."

"How are—how are you?"

"I'm fine. That never happens. What happened. That was an aberration. That means it was an unusual occurrence and out of the ordinary."

"I know what *aberration* means," I say. At least I do now. "And I know it wasn't usual."

He keeps scrolling through articles. "And I didn't— it didn't last long. I know how to—usually, I can feel what I feel and I'm fine. But sometimes it's harder. It hasn't happened in a long time. Just yesterday. Because… just because."

"You don't have to explain," I say. I'd hate it if I felt like I had to explain my Jenga moments. "It's okay."

"Okay."

"So… do you want to hear something awesome?"

"I'm busy."

I think he's embarrassed even though his face doesn't give anything away. And I realize he's the opposite of

Briggs. But if Briggs wears his heart on his sleeve, I wonder where Will wears his? Maybe on his lists?

I want him to know it's okay. And I know one way to make him feel better.

"I have information," I say.

"What kind of information?"

"Oh, just information on the one thing you want in the world." I can't help it. I'm grinning.

Will begins scrolling online again. "You know there's nothing I want information on except how to get inside the Leland estate."

I don't answer. Instead I begin humming my awesome would-be theme song to myself and setting my lunch out.

"Wait." Will looks over at me and then back down. "You're smiling. Why are you smiling? Are you joking or do you actually have information on the Leland estate? I can't tell. You need to tell me."

I take an extra minute to open up my water bottle and take a deep, deep drink. It's cold and delicious. And oh-so-satisfying.

I lean in toward him and say, "You're going to want to get out that list."

Chapter 35

Leland Labyrinth

1) <u>1928</u>: Henry Leland III buys Horse's Neck, an 1,800-acre peninsula on the North Shore of Long Island, and builds the famous Leland estate on the northern tip by the water.

2) <u>1961</u>: His son, Henry Leland IV, keeps 600 acres around the estate for himself and

sells the remaining 1,200 acres to the state. NY State turns the land into Cauffield State Park.

Mr. Leland builds a huge stone wall around his 600 acres and lives there in seclusion. Rumors spread that he is building one of the country's biggest labyrinths, which will not be opened to the public.

3) <u>This year</u>: A rare photograph of the famous Leland greenhouse appears in *American Architect* magazine. The entrance of the labyrinth can be seen in the distance.

An original map of the 1928 estate property plans will show the path to the greenhouse.

4) There is currently a damaged section of the famous outer wall that surrounds the Leland estate. This piece of information was discovered by Beatrix Lee, who insisted that this be noted despite the fact that no

sources have been noted for the rest of the information.

Conclusion:

We will find the damaged part of wall and enter through this section. Then we will follow the map to the greenhouse. This will ultimately lead to the labyrinth.

Potential Problem:

Killer Hounds

I can't help it. I'm feeling a little…smug. Even though he didn't say it, I bet Will was pretty impressed when I told him about the whole adventure and how Old Man Leland was even scarier in person and how Jenny Leland was so nice to me even after I almost ran out of the elevator. I sit back and wait for him to let me know how much he appreciates all my efforts.

"Just go ahead and say it! THANK YOU, O GREAT

BEA. I mean, isn't the list so much better now that you have my life-changing and vital information added?" I nudge him. "Oh, and I know a couple of paths where we can sneak into the park without using the front entrance. Add that!"

"Yes," agrees Will. "THANK YOU. Your information is vital. But why do we need another path when there's a main entrance with a road that leads straight to the Leland property?"

"Well...don't you think it's important to—you know—Go Stealth?" I say. S finds her way even into this mission. But I can't help that.

"Why?"

I turn and point out the window where you can see the soccer field. "It's kind of like...like when I sneak out of school. Aren't you less likely to know what I'm up to if I sneak around the edges instead of sprinting down the middle of the soccer field? Plus, when you go in the main entrance, the park ranger knows you're in there. I think the fewer people we see, the better."

"I like that."

"You do?"

"Yes. You should give me a list of all the paths that

lead into the park, and I can figure out which one is the best."

"Okay!" I say. This is a good day for me. I'm a provider of vital information and ideas. "We just need one last little piece of information."

"We need to know when those masons are coming," Will says. "What was the name of the company? We can call them and find out their schedule."

"I don't remember—like the Windy City Masons or something," I say. "But that doesn't matter. I know who can tell us and I have her number and an invitation to call anytime I want."

"Jenny Leland."

"Jenny. Of the Pink Heels. Leland." I pick up my phone. "I already figured out how to ask her—and just think, you get to watch it all happen live."

The phone barely rings once.

"Yes! Hello! Jenny Leland speaking!"

I look at Will and grin. "Hi, Jenny! It's Beatrix, Eve Lee's daughter—"

"Bea! Hi! How are you? Nice to hear from you so soon. How did things work out with your friend? Will, right?"

"Oh, Will's fine." I wink at him. "He decided to find another labyrinth. So he's happy."

"I'm glad. So how can I help you? I do have a meeting in a few minutes—"

"No, no, that's fine, I just wanted to ask about those, um, Windy City masons?"

"Kanakaris Masonry? The ones doing my uncle's wall?"

I recite the story I planned. "Yes. Well, my mom and dad are going to build this wall for privacy on our property, but when I told my mom that you had these special masons coming, she got all excited—you know, being an artist and everything—and she thought it would be great to have, like, a really beautiful wall. So maybe while they're here, she can talk to them?"

Jenny pauses on the other end. "Well, planning something like a wall is a big job, Bea. It's not exactly something they could just squeeze in. I think your parents would be better off finding someone local—"

"It's just that my mom is crazy about—your uncle's, um, his...style...." I say a secret apology to my mom in my head. "She thinks he has really great...taste. She's just crazy about the wall around the property...."

"Really? Wow...that surprises me....I wouldn't have guessed that the whole ancient Greek stone look was her thing...."

"It is, actually. Totally her thing. So maybe the Windy City guys could just stop by and talk to her. If you told me the *exact dates* they were coming to do that repair, then I could see if my mom could have them over—"

"It's just such short notice, Bea. They'll be here Monday and my uncle's coming back that same day— honestly, he won't be happy with anyone else taking up their time. Even your mom."

"Oh!" I look straight at Will. "So...Mr. Leland... your uncle is away right now?" I try to keep my voice low, and I say the words as clearly as I can. Will leans forward.

"Just till Monday."

"Just till Monday," I say. Something else occurs to me. Something big. "He must—I bet he probably puts his, um, his dogs in some fancy dog hotel while he's gone, huh? I mean, I hear he really worships them." I try to joke. "Haha, reservations at the Doggy Plaza?"

Jenny laughs. "You're a riot, Bea. I hate to say it, but both Doggy Plaza and 'worship' are terrifyingly on target. That man would fill an entire museum with doggy statues if he could. Listen, I'd love to chat more, Bea, but I really have to run and finish up a few things. If Uncle Henry says he'll be back first thing Monday, he means it. That man does not like to change plans."

Another thing he has in common with Will.

"Sorry I couldn't be more help."

"No, actually you were a huge help!"

"I was?"

"I mean—thanks for always being so nice, Jenny."

"Aw. You're welcome, Bea. Say hi to your mom and to Will for me."

"I will."

"Bye, now!"

I hang up. "Did you hear that? Mr. Leland is out of town, and the Killer Hounds are out of the picture."

Will is staring intently at the list. Pencil poised. Ready to add more information. "I could only hear your side of the conversation. What else did she say? I need you to tell me everything. Who are these masons and what are the exact dates again? I want to check everything on the list."

"The Windy City masons arrive from the Windy

City on Monday—check! Old Man Leland is out of town till Monday—check! Killer Hounds are at the Doggy Plaza till Monday—check!"

"That's it? Jenny Leland didn't say anything else? Details are important."

"Well, she did say to say hi to you. So...Hi, Will! Check!"

"Okay, then, today's Tuesday. We'll bike up there right after school and find the weak spot. When I see it, I'll have a better idea for a plan. Then we have three days to practice—Wednesday, Thursday, Friday. This means that we can go on Saturday or Sunday."

"Oh." Bike there today? And go Saturday or Sunday. It seems so soon. Maybe we need more information. I don't want to mess up our one chance. "Wait. Shouldn't we talk about this more? Are three days of practice enough? What if Mr. Leland changes his flight? What if the masons come early? What if—"

Will shakes his head. "Stop. Everything is lined up just right. We have to do it now. After Mr. Leland fixes the wall, we'll have to start over with a new plan. When else are we going to get a chance like this?"

Of course, he's right.

"You're right," I say.

"I know," Will replies.

"Only … it's too bad. …"

"What's too bad? There's nothing bad. …"

"It'll be after the date. … November eleventh will have passed. So no more eleventh day on the eleventh month kind of thing."

Will pauses. "That's not the important part."

"It's not?"

"No, the important part is that we're doing it."

We.

"You're right," I say again.

"I know," Will replies again.

Chapter 36

The sun has been going down earlier and earlier since the beginning of November and now sets just a little after 4:30 PM. Right after school, we head straight home to get our bikes. School officially ends at 2:20 PM. That gives us just two hours. I know I can make it to the park in less than half an hour from my house.

Six hundred acres of property sounds bigger than I can imagine. Especially when I know that our family has two acres and everyone thinks that's huge. I don't see anyone as I zoom through the park. Not as many people come this time of year when it starts getting cold. When I get to the edge of the Leland estate, Will is just ahead of me. There are several trails and roads inside the park that lead here. He must have taken a different one or I would've seen him on the way in.

He looks at his watch and nods at me when I ride up.

"I should switch the path I take so we can ride to the wall together. Or you can switch to mine. Or we could meet on the road before the paths. Or what if—"

"Stop." Will shakes his head. "You keep doing that. We both got here at the same time. Just do the same thing you did today. That's all that matters. We have to find the weak spot. We have an hour."

"Fine."

"Fine."

Luck is on our side. We don't even need the whole hour.

The weak spot couldn't have been more perfectly placed. Toward the far right edge of the property, around a curve in the wall where no one would really notice it unless they were looking. We just happen to be the ones looking.

I have never been up close to the famous wall that protects the Leland estate from the rest of the park. Everyone says it's like a fortress, but when I look at it, I see there is no mortar or cement or glue or anything between the stones. It's pretty amazing. I mean, how do things stay together like that when there isn't anything actually holding them?

The damage was caused by this huge fallen tree. A lot of the tree has already been cleared, except for a big part of the trunk, which is lying inside the wall. But it won't be a problem to get around. Someone has blocked the opening with a rusty piece of chicken wire.

Will and I start adding to the list. And the next part of the plan comes together.

We need tools. To bend back the chicken wire.

Will can get the right ones from home.

We need something so we won't scratch ourselves on the sharp edges.

I could bring an old towel or newspapers.

We find places to hide the bikes. Thick yew bushes near the opening for Will and farther around the corner for me.

We peek through the chicken wire. If only we had

216

time to go in today and explore a little so we could get a feeling for exactly where the labyrinth is. But it's too risky this close to sunset.

"We won't have enough time to look for the labyrinth till Saturday," Will says. "Then we'll have all day."

"And if that doesn't work, then we still have Sunday, so we have options," I say. "It's going to happen!" I close my eyes and try to imagine the green walls and turning paths. "What do you think it'll be like inside?"

Will stays perfectly still, staring through the chicken wire. He doesn't answer.

But I know what he's thinking.

"Well, just promise me you'll wear a coat," I say, shivering. This fall has been cold and Will is still only wearing his thin striped T-shirt.

"I already told you I don't like coats. They're itchy and they always have tags."

"Just cut the tags out!" I say.

He shakes his head. "Then the sharp edge will stab me in the back of the neck. No. Biking will keep me warm on the way here and walking the path will keep me warm inside and then I'll be biking back."

"But, Will—"

"I told you: I don't want to carry anything with me. No phone. No coat. Nothing. I want to walk—just walk."

Walk Just Walk.

If you think about it, it sounds pretty nice. No baggage or burdens or itchy coats and a winding Zen path to calm you as you go. Will's way might not be that bad.

"Okay," I say. "We'll walk—just walk."

We'll Walk Just Walk together.

Chapter 37

On Saturday, I bike as fast as I can to meet Will at the Leland estate. Today might be the day. Positive thinking! Today IS the day! Each pump of my pedal is bringing me closer and closer.

I hear it before I can see it.

A roar.

Voices.

I make the final turn, and Will is standing with his bike on the road watching a small army of trucks and at least a dozen men, who are all talking and moving around.

No! No! No!

My heart is pounding. They aren't supposed to be here until Monday.

I zoom up to Will. "Oh no!" I cry. "Why are they here? It's only Saturday! How did this happen?"

Will turns to me. "Stop that. What are you yelling about?"

"The Windy City guys!" I point to the trucks. But then I see one says NORTH SHORE LANDSCAPING. Another says TREE TOP TREE SERVICE. The roar is chain saws.

"You have to stop being anxious all the time," he says. "It doesn't help." But when he looks at his watch, he nods. I may be dramatic, but at least I'm always on time. "They're cutting up the tree trunk today," he says. "I've been listening to them talking." I can tell he's in Information Gathering Mode. "The other men are gardening. A fall cleanup, they called it. They're going to be here all day."

I think about it. "I guess it's noisy and messy and Mr. Leland wanted it all done while he was away."

"They're going to be here till dark. I heard Blue Baseball Hat arguing with Yellow Vest. He doesn't want to come in on Sunday, too, but they have one small job to finish. Yellow Vest says he'll come with just one truck and be done by one PM."

1:00 PM. That gives us two more hours than we had when we came from school, but it's very different from having all day. I follow Will down the road back into the main part of the park. He stops and rests his bike at a bench.

"We'll meet right inside the wall at one thirty. That'll give them enough time to leave."

"I don't know. Is that enough time? How about I'll meet you inside the labyrinth instead? I think we should just try to get there as soon as we can. I mean, what if one of us is late or delayed or something happ—"

"Why do you always talk about all the things that *might* go wrong? It doesn't help. It never helps."

"But the sun sets before five, Will. We'll already be starting late. Think about it. I'll meet you inside the labyrinth—"

"You need to stop. You're not helping," Will says. "No one is going to be late."

"You stop. I *am* helping. If we figure out all the things that can go wrong, we can be better prepared."

How can he say I'm not helping? I've been a huge help.

Will would probably still be sitting all alone in the *Broadside* office just dreaming about getting into the Leland estate if I hadn't been such a huge help. I take a deep breath. Okay. This is Will. He just needs to hear the reasons.

"Will. I know you get—you get weird when things change, but all I'm saying is we should plan, just in case—"

"Stop talking like I'm the problem. I'm not the problem. You are."

My mouth drops open. "How am I the—I'm just trying—"

"You're the problem because you want to change everything and we've already figured it out. You get scared that things won't work out—you're always scared. Everyone has a weakness. That's yours—and that's the problem."

"That's so unfair! I'm not afraid of—I'm the one who went into the city to ask Mr. Leland—the meanest man on the planet—for information! For you!"

"You said you were too afraid to talk to him and you ran out of the elevator. Jenny Leland's the only reason you have any information. You didn't get it. She gave it to you."

Why, why, why does Will's superpower have to be the ability to remember everything?

"Well, would someone who's afraid just get up and leave school whenever they want? I cut classes all the time—"

"That's just running away again. My cousin told me how you ran out of class."

"Your cousin—Dan Ross? You talked to—to *Dan Ross*—about me?"

"Dan Ross is my cousin—"

"I *know* he's your cousin! Why would you—why would you talk to him—about me?"

"We had dinner at my aunt's house. Dan said you were crying over a rat and you ran away. He said you're afraid of everything—you've been that way since kindergarten—"

"Hammy's not a rat! Dan Ross is the rat—Hammy's a hamster and you weren't even there."

Will continues as if I haven't spoken. "And you're afraid of those girls."

"What…girls."

But I know what girls.

"Those girls who aren't your friends. The ones you're

223

always looking at who never look at you. The ones you're afraid to talk to."

I have no answer.

Will doesn't even look like he cares. He's studying his handlebars. "You're afraid to talk to them because they don't want to be friends with you. I hear them talk about it. You say I'm weird, but they think you are. You should be glad to have this information, so you can just walk away. People don't like people who don't fit in. I don't fit in. You don't, either. So it makes sense that we don't have friends."

I can't see because my eyes have gone blurry, and I'm not sure what's filling them with tears: the fact that Will says he heard the girls talking about me or that he says neither of us has friends. Because if neither of us has friends, it means we're not even friends with each other.

"I'm not…" But I can't finish the sentence. Because Will has already added in all the necessary information. There's only one conclusion to draw.

In Taiwan, when I stood on the diving board, I dove in even though I was afraid. Even though the water looked like a solid blue wall that would smash me to pieces. I did it because I had people behind me, cheering. But this whole thing with Will is a dive I never should've taken. Because it's smashed me beyond repair.

He's right.

We don't have friends.

He's just someone who happened to be in an office I ran into. Because I was running away. From the cafeteria and S and A and all the things I heard them say.

I stumble as I walk my bike away. I'll pedal as soon as I can see again.

"We'll meet inside the wall at one thirty PM," I hear Will saying behind me. "That's the plan. It will give us plenty of time. Stick to the plan."

I don't say a word.

What is there to say?

I'm no one and nothing to anyone.

Not even to a boy in a striped shirt.

Chapter 38

I don't remember the ride home. I don't remember if I put my bike back neatly in the garage or just dropped it on the driveway. And I don't remember how long I've been standing here outside my parents' studio.

I wonder what Will's doing.

If he got home safe.

Of course he did. He doesn't need me. He's probably busy making lists. That's what he does. He made one about me. I thought it was about how to be friends, but maybe his lists are about whatever's in front of him—whatever problem he has to figure out—and I'm just one of those problems. A problem that interrupted his safe Zen place.

I'm not part of the safety. I'm part of the interruption.

I lean my forehead against the coolness of the studio door. I don't want to be part of the interruption here, too. I let my hand linger on the dragon.

And then push.

The door opens without a sound. Maybe I can hide in the entrance for a little bit. My parents probably won't even be coming into the house tonight. Not with how busy they are.

With Mom's show that's all about flying through the sky with her new baby.

And Dad's movie that's all about his and Mom's combined superpowers.

I peek in.

Mom is in the middle of the room.

Crying.

I almost run to her, because it makes no sense. She never cries. She's joyful and unstoppable. I see my dad pacing and talking and I stay hidden and listen.

"...and you'll find another gallery."

Mom cries harder.

"We can even start contacting places tomorrow...."

She covers her face with her hands.

"I can find the ones who've reached out to you before—"

Mom bursts into fresh tears.

"What else can I—" Dad stands there, helpless.

She just keeps crying.

She won't stop and Dad doesn't know what to do and I don't, either. How do you help someone if you can't read their Look or hear the words inside their head or ... just don't see them because they're invisible? What can anyone ever do? How does it ever get better?

Then Mom looks up, still crying, and just holds her arms out.

Dad goes to her and wraps himself around her and just holds her and holds her and doesn't say another word. And the answer comes to me:

No one can ever really know what you want.

Even if you wish it more than anything in the world, they can never know...

unless

I step inside.

They look up right away.

Dad clears his throat. "We just need a minute, Trix. Why don't you go back to the house and—"

I shake my head and take another step.

"Trix?" Mom wipes her face and looks at me. "Are you okay?"

I open my mouth. And then close it.

And then open it again.

My voice is tiny. But it's there.

"I want—I want us to be together more—"

Mom starts toward me, but my hand goes up and she stops.

I can feel my eyes begin to fill. "And I *know* you want me to be all independent—and responsible— and I *know* you're busy—I mean, I really know, know, *know* you're busy—but you're always in here—and I'm always—"

Alone. At school. Alone. On the path. Alone. In my blank-walled room.

"I'm always—alone."

The thing about saying words that used to only be in

your head is that when they come out, each one becomes like a stepping-stone in a path you never knew was there.

I step again.

And the tears begin to spill.

"And I just—I don't feel like I'm part of anything—"

Dad shakes his head. "You are—you're part of everything—"

No. "Mom has her show and you have your movie and—"

"Oh, Trix..." Dad looks at the space still between us. "You're part of the movie. You're the biggest part. Where do you think Sky came from?"

I wipe my eyes. "You and Mom."

Dad's laugh is a small huff of air as he and Mom look at each other. Then me. "You're kind of right," he says. "You know that—that Sky is *you*, right?"

"Me?"

I don't remember walking those last few steps, and I can't see anything because I'm blinded by tears, but I'm suddenly standing right in front of them both. Like something inside me just knew the way to go.

Dad reaches out. He holds my chin so he can look me in the eyes. His are shiny and dark behind his glasses. "Do you know anyone else who writes things in the sky?"

Something is happening inside me. It's like when you're searching and searching for the right song that feels exactly the way you want to feel and then when you find it, it fills you up so much that it spills out and just flows everywhere around you and you can't believe how lucky you are to be in a world where there is music.

And then I am in the middle of arms and a round belly pressed against me and kisses on my head. "We're going to be together more—we're sorry," Mom whispers into my hair.

"We promise," Dad says. "No matter what—and if we forget, tell us—just tell us. But we won't forget."

And then Dad begins to hum the song he dances to with Mom, but this time, we all dance together as a family. The three of us. And I am in the middle of it and no one is letting me go.

I don't say anything more.

I guess that's the other thing about words that you let out. When they form enough of a path, you get to a place where sometimes you don't have to say anything at all.

Chapter 39

The next day, the house is quiet. I'm in my room and it's Sunday, Leland Labyrinth Day.

And Will needs me.

He might not say the words, but I know he does. And I'm going to be there for him. I check the time and smile. If I get out of here in the next ten minutes, I'll even be ahead of schedule.

I woke up early, getting a few things ready and trying to stay as quiet as possible, so Mom and Dad would sleep in. I haven't heard anything yet, so they're either still sleeping or in the studio. Usually, I don't have to explain anything to them if I disappear all day. I can just sneak off and leave a note like *Went for a bike ride! Be back soon! I love you!* I can even decorate it with curls and swirls and little drawings of chickadees and dancing mongoose (mongeese?), which would make Mom so happy. But I think I'll at least tell them I'll be up on the Neck and won't have cell service. This way they won't try to call me and they won't worry if they don't hear from me.

I'm picking out colors for my note when I hear Mom yell, "Time to go!"

Oh no. She is up. And in the house. And doing her classic mental health day roll call. I should have known this would happen after I asked them to spend more time with me yesterday. On any other day there would be nothing I'd want more than to spend time with my mom and dad in the city. But today, I have to be with Will. How do I tell her?

I stick my head out of my room.

"Mom? I can't go anywhere. I have—I have a thing

with—" I hate to say it, but I don't know what else to do. "The girls. I promised. We're biking up on the Neck. I'm running out right now."

Dad peeks up the stairs. "Where're you going?"

I take a quick breath and try to sound casual. I didn't know he was up, too. "Oh, I'm meeting the girls. We're going to bike up to the Neck, so—"

Mom appears. Clutching her belly.

I see that Dad has a small rolling suitcase behind him. "I have everything ready—though I'm pretty sure there're only paints and brushes in here." Then he looks at Mom. "I know you want to walk to the hospital, but I am starting up the car in two seconds."

Wait.

Wait. Wait. WAIT.

I stare at Mom. "Do you mean time to go like it's TIME-time? Like baby time?"

Mom gives her belly a pat. "It's two weeks early, but Starling's been at it all morning."

Dad beckons to her. "C'mon, let's get you in the car."

"No way. Forget the car. I have a plan. You know I have a plan. I'm walking," Mom says. "It's less than two miles into town. I want us to walk the path hand in hand toward this as a family." She looks at me. "Don't forget I walked six miles the day I was in labor with the Trix! All over the city!"

Dad shakes his head. "Uh, walking six miles was what put you into labor. We had to jump in a cab and rush to the hospital! No walking today."

"You'll walk with me, won't you, Trixie?" Mom dimples at me.

"Do not try to sway her with your magic spells." Dad laughs. "We are not walking. It's cold out. Let's just drive. And let Trix play with her friends. She's hardly been with them all year."

I look up at Dad. I didn't realize anyone had noticed.

"Besides, it'll take hours," he says. "And she's not allowed in the delivery room. I like that Trix has somewhere to go instead of waiting in the hospital all day. She can check in now and then and zip over or one of the parents can drive her."

My mind is racing.

I want to be with my mom and I want us to be together as a family. But I also need to be with Will. I check the time again. I bet I can do both.

"Mom, I'm with Dad. It's too cold and also you just

235

need to get there fast. So let's drive. I can put my bike in the back, since I...I promised the girls I would hang out and bike today. And, like Dad said, in case you have to stay late, I can just stay with them."

Mom smiles. "I love that," she says. "But promise you won't take the busy street by the hospital. Go around the block."

"There are bike lanes on every road in this town. She can handle it," Dad says. He points at me. "Just be off the road before it gets dark. Now, I'm going to run this out to the car, which means you have exactly three minutes. Go, go, go!"

I'm already dressed in warm layers. I run upstairs and grab my backpack, turning it upside down and shaking everything out on the floor. Will doesn't want to bring anything. He wants to Walk Just Walk. But I'm going to carry my backpack. Because I want to put something special inside for him. My dad's softest flannel jacket. I carefully took the label out—every stitch so there's not even the trace of itch left. And I'm bringing two thermoses of hot chocolate. The right brand. No marshmallows. When we get to the ultimate Zen center,

I want us to sit and drink them together. I rush down to the kitchen, where I have them ready to go.

"Ready, Mom?" I call.

"Ready!" Mom yells.

Dad pops back in. "Ready! By the way, Trix, just saw the girls ride by when I was putting Mom's suitcase in the car—"

My heart stops. "What?"

"Don't worry, I told them we had to go to the hospital first and that you would meet them as soon as you could—"

No.

"You—what?"

He dances over to Mom, then dips her and pretends to stagger under the weight. They both laugh as if my head has not just exploded. "I told them you had some serious big-sister duties first—and I may have laughed when I said *duties*. Anyway, I said you'd call them as soon as Mom was settled in the hospital."

No.

No, no, no, no, no.

"Dad—you didn't. Tell me you didn't."

"They thought it was funny. *Duties*."

"That's not even what I—"

"Who's the tall girl with them?"

A was there.

Of course.

I feel faint. "It doesn't matter. She's—she's no one."

Mom looks at me. "That's not nice, Trix."

"I didn't mean—I'm just nervous and excited, Mom. That's all...." I finish up lamely.

Dad hustles us into the car and I think about how he always picks S up and swings her around in a circle when he sees her.

Please, please, please tell me that did not happen.

As we turn onto Main Street, all the lights are green and Dad hoots with laughter and zooms through. A song comes on the radio, and Dad turns it way up, and even though it's freezing out, he rolls down the windows and he and Mom look at each other and sing so everyone on the sidewalks can hear them.

Maybe I should text S and say something like:

my dad told me he said the weirdest thing to you today—poor guy hasn't slept in days w his big movie coming up

Or do I just ignore it? I haven't sent her a text since the first day of school.

Are they talking about me now?

Or even worse ... Does A think I'm trying to squeeze my way into their group? Or that I'm lying to my parents so they think I still have friends?

The song Mom and Dad are singing is telling me things, but I don't believe them. It doesn't feel like anything is going to get any easier. But I close my eyes and listen anyway, resting my chin on the window, feeling the cold on my face as my hair flies loose in the wind like streamers.

The drive is only a few minutes. Dad parks in the lot and then offers Mom his arm, shouting, "Lady with a baby, coming through!" as we enter the building.

Some people come running over with a wheelchair and make Mom sit in it even though she swears she can still walk a mile. Then we have to go through filling out paperwork and talking to every doctor on the planet.

I look up at the clock on the wall. Great. Now I'm going to be late. After all this, now I'll have Will mad at me. Well, not mad. Will doesn't get mad. He gets factual and lecture-y. I can already picture him, waiting inside the wall with his arms crossed. How many times has he told me he hates to wait? At least, I can tell him my mom is about to have her baby. That'll shut him up. It's the one thing I don't think he'll have one of his answers for.

"Mom," I say. "I think I'm going to go now. I mean, it's okay, right? You said it takes hours?"

Mom squeezes me. "Hours. And how is that middle name coming?"

"Oh. I . . . still haven't decided."

"Okay, Starling's not here yet, but when she is, she's going to want one. Get me a cup of ice before you go, Trix?"

I plant a kiss on her forehead. "Yes, of course." I run over to the side table where the pitcher and cups are.

Mom's doctor comes in and gives my parents a huge hello. She's all out of breath. "Just delivered twins! A boy and a girl—sorry to keep you waiting."

"Oh, I'm used to waiting." Mom looks at Dad. "What? You're late for everything. Everything!"

"Total exaggeration," Dad says. "You are the late

one. Or you would be if you ever had to commute any farther than your studio. Trix is the only one in this family who's never late."

"True," Mom says. "We're hopeless. Trix is the grown-up."

I laugh. It's almost true. And what they don't know about me being late for Mr. Clarke's class every day won't hurt them.

"I don't think she's ever been more than five minutes late for anything," Mom brags. "Unless she's just not coming. With Trix, she's either on time or she's a no-show."

There's a crash as I drop the cup of ice.

"I . . ."

I grab napkins and try to clean up. The nurse comes over.

"I have it, sweetheart. Don't get all upset, it's just ice."

But it's not.

It's not just ice.

It's Will. Waiting for me.

Will, who looks at his watch whenever I arrive for lunch. And every day this week at the Leland estate. Looking at his watch and nodding because I'm always on time. Always.

But not today.

This important day.

As far as he knows right now, I'm a no-show.

And I can't stop thinking about what happened that last time someone was a no-show. Only this time, there's no Mrs. Reegs or safe place for Will at the Leland estate. He's all alone.

Chapter 40

"Trix, are you okay?" Mom asks. "I don't want you riding around if you're upset. The girls will be fine if you're late. Or Dad can drive you. Maybe you shouldn't go; it gets dark early."

"No, no, I'm fine. I just—the cup slipped and it shocked me and I can ride my bike. Besides, we're supposed to go bike riding together, so it wouldn't make sense to be driven there. But if it starts to get dark, we'll just...hang out at the house. Okay?"

I kiss her and hug her extra tight, ready to bolt out

the door. But then I have to wait for my dad to come with me so he can get the bike out of the back of the Jeep. And we go to the wrong parking area twice, and by the time I'm on my bike I'm already way beyond late. I try Will's cell phone, but it goes to voice mail. Of course. He's already in the no-cell zone. I know this, but I still leave a message. It's the only thing I can do.

"Will, it's me. It's Bea. I'm coming, so don't—I don't want you to worry, okay? I'll be there. Just wait for me."

But I know he won't get it.

Because Will would never be late. He's been practicing and practicing and has it down to a T. He's already there.

Chapter 41

When a bike tire goes flat, it's not a big *pop*. Or even a long, slow hiss like in a cartoon. It just sounds...different.

Will insisted that part of the plan should be to double-check our bikes, and I ignored that part because it seemed silly. I've never checked my bike for anything in my life. I don't even know how to check a bike. And now here I am, and once again, Will was right.

I know I can't call my dad because he needs to be with my mom, and I can't call Mrs. Reegs because I don't think she'd appreciate that I'm helping a student break into a crazy billionaire's home, and I can't call the one person I've called most of my life in a crisis because she's somewhere with A and L and L wondering why my dad just told them I was going to go bike riding with them. And that's not even something I want to begin to think about. So there really isn't anyone else I can even imagine calling.

Except...maybe there is.

I have the number.

Mrs. Reegs gave it to me, along with everyone else's at the *Broadside*. Just in case. I think this just might be one of those cases.

And I know he's good at fixing things and I really, really need help fixing not only my bike, but this whole day. And I don't even have time to think about how if I call Briggs, he's going to think it's like a *call*-call. I guess it doesn't even matter. I drag my bike to the side of the road and lean it against a tree. Then I pull out my phone. I have to walk way back in the opposite direction until I have cell service again.

After three rings, he picks up. "Um, hi..."

I take a breath, but nothing comes out.

"...Bea? Is that you? Or is this a butt dial? Hello?"

Silence.

"Are you okay?"

I shake my head.

"Bea?"

I take a deep breath. "I'm sorry, Briggs. I need help."

Briggs rides up on his bike twenty-seven minutes later. His street is on the far end of the paths, and I realize that this means he must have left his house the second he got off the phone with me. I add this to a list of things about Briggs I've started in my head. I'm jogging in place when he arrives because now that I'm not biking, I'm really feeling the cold.

"I'm sorry," I say right away. "I didn't know who else to call."

"You don't have to keep saying *sorry*," says Briggs. "It's okay. But why didn't you call your parents to pick you up? I mean, I'm glad you called me, it's just..."

At least I don't have to lie about this. "They're both at the hospital. My mom's having her baby. Will's waiting for me and, um, Mr. Leland is expecting us, and I don't know anyone who drives. So I thought you could help me fix my bike—or if you can't—and if you don't mind—maybe we could . . . ride double on yours. Sorry, I know that means more work for you." I feel my cheeks go hot. I definitely don't want Briggs to think this is all a plan just to ride double with him. I mean, will I have to hold on to him the whole time?

Briggs blushes. "No, I'm glad you called me—it's just that I don't have a spare tire." He blushes a little deeper. "But I don't mind riding double. I mean, at least it's a good way to keep warm." Then he smiles at me in this sweet awkward way that makes me wish people didn't have to start *liking* people in a way that wasn't just friendship. Because I just really, really like Briggs.

When you ride double, the person in the front does all the work, pedaling. The other person sits on the seat and lets their legs just hang. You don't have to hold on to the pedaling person if you don't want to. You can just hold on to your seat as long as you stay balanced.

As soon as we set off, I can tell that Briggs is a strong

biker—which I like because he sort of looks like the kind of person who stays in and reads all day. I think we might even get there faster than if I were alone. Even though I can feel we're in perfect balance, I still hang on tight to him as we bike down the road.

Chapter 42

"Hold on!" Briggs shouts into the wind as we swoop down the last long, winding hill before the edge of the Leland estate. My hair flies behind me, and for a second, I forget everything and smile. He had to ride the last mile with one hand on top of his head after his hat flew off and we had to rush back and get it.

We come to a stop by a large green sign with gold letters. I put my feet on the ground and slide off.

LELAND ESTATE
THIS IS PRIVATE PROPERTY.
NO TRESPASSING.
NO PUBLIC ACCESS.
NO PARK PATRONS.
PLEASE RESPECT OUR PRIVACY.

Briggs is flushed and smiling. "So, now what? Does a butler come out and get us?" His smile drops when he sees my face. "What? Are you okay?"

"I'm fine. It's just...Mr. Leland...he's not expecting...us both." I feel terrible as the words come out.

"Oh." And now I feel even worse.

"Also, he told me that—that he has a migraine, so I shouldn't ring the bell or the intercom or anything. Because then—the dogs—the Killer Hounds—go crazy and start barking—and the noise..."

"It's okay...."

I may be the worst person in the world. Briggs rode all the way out here to help me. He brought me right up to the gate. And now I'm hinting that he needs to go. I try not to think how I had that little moment of happiness swooping down the hill, riding double with him. He might not want to be my friend if he finds out about all the lies. But I don't know what else to do, so I keep on lying.

"I want you to come—I do. It's just that he was really...stern and mysterious about calling or ringing the doorbell or anything," I add for drama. "Remember, you were saying before about how private he is. Old Man Leland." I force my mouth into a smile.

Briggs nods. "Okay. So, I guess you could just text him."

I panic for a second and then remember. "Actually, there's no cell service here." I hold up my phone as proof. "You know, the whole Neck is like this...."

Briggs looks at me funny. "Then how are you supposed to get in to see the labyrinth and meet up with Will?"

I take a deep breath and start walking along the wall toward the opening. I steal a quick glance at the bushes where Will was supposed to hide his bike and—it's there! That means he's in. But whether he's waiting just inside or walking calmly without me...or upset somewhere, I don't know.

"So, Mr. Leland said it would probably be easiest if I just slipped through this part of the wall that got damaged—it's just up ahead. Plus, this way I don't have to go through the whole, you know, fancy-schmancy being-announced-by-the-butler thing. It's just so weird, isn't it?"

I keep edging forward and Briggs keeps following.

"That . . . is weird," he says.

I look through the opening covered with the scrap of rusted fence. No more fallen tree. Stones lying around the collapsed part of the wall. Will's pliers and the newspaper lie near my feet. He must have thrown them over after he bent the fence back.

I peer through, hoping I'll see Will just on the other side. Maybe mad and ready to lecture me on lateness and the importance of plans, which I would gladly listen to right now. But he's nowhere in sight.

I check the road. Empty. I have to hurry. I'll get in and ditch Briggs and then run as fast as I can to get to Will.

"Can you help me for a sec?" I hand Briggs the pliers and he bends the fence back out of the way while I hold it with the newspaper. I carefully climb through and let out a big breath when I get to the other side. Just inside the wall, behind the big stone, is Will's phone. *I don't want to carry anything with me. No phone. No coat. Nothing. I want to walk—just walk.*

I give my backpack a pat and feel the big comfy coat I have inside. He may want to Walk Just Walk, but I will not let him freeze just freeze. I look at his phone lying there all alone and I put mine next to his. I don't know where he is right now, but at least my phone can keep his company. We wouldn't even be able to use them around here if we wanted. I brush my hands off and turn back to Briggs.

"So, anyway, thanks again. Um, I guess I'll see you in school—"

Briggs is standing on the outside of the wall, looking back and forth from the pliers to the bent chicken wire.

"Wait. Mr. Leland—Old Man Leland—told you to come here and slip through the—with the rust and the—" He stops and looks up at me, his eyes big. "You aren't even invited here, are you?" The pliers fall to the ground. "You—you just had me help you break into—I just broke into the property of a billionaire. With Killer Hounds."

He searches my face.

"You lied to me?"

I open my mouth, but nothing comes out. And even if anything did, the way Briggs is looking at me, I'm not sure he'd believe me.

Chapter 43

I try to gulp in the cold air, but I feel like I'm choking.

"I—I'm sorry," I say.

For the first time, Briggs doesn't tell me not to be.

I feel miserable. "Yes, I lied. Will and I didn't get permission to be here. At all. Not even close. Mr. Leland wouldn't even talk to me. I'm so sorry, Briggs. I was supposed to be here, but I'm late." I stumble back close to the opening and look at Briggs. "I'm late and I'm afraid Will is...in there somewhere thinking I just didn't show up. Like that day at the *Broadside*."

Briggs nods, his straight brows coming together in concern.

"I didn't know what else to do. I had to call someone for help and now you probably won't even want to be friends with me—and—and the Windy City whatevers are coming and Will is probably in there all alone and—"

Will had said I don't have any friends.

But I do.

He's my friend and I don't want him to think I'm a no-show. That this wasn't important enough for me to be there. Because it was—it is. It's the most important thing.

"No one's even seen us here—you can just take off on your bike and no one will ever know—and even if I get caught, I swear I won't tell anyone you helped. I can wipe your fingerprints off the pliers—and—and if they hook me up to one of those lie detector tests, I'll just— I'll just—what are you..." Briggs has begun to climb through the opening. "What are you doing?"

He stands in front of me. "I'm coming." He straightens his fedora. "I want to help."

Briggs is coming with me? After everything I just

said and did? A tiny ray of hope shoots through me. I won't have to wander the Leland estate alone.

"You are? Even though I—and you don't even—really?"

Briggs looks at me. "Just tell me one thing...."

"Anything!"

And then he smiles his whole-face smile. "What's a Windy City whatever?"

I don't care what kind of way Briggs likes me, or what he or anyone thinks, I lunge right at him and throw my arms around his neck and hug him as tight as I can. "Can I tell you on the way?"

I didn't think it was possible, but Briggs has blushed even redder. He pats me on the back, but he kind of laughs, too.

"Deal," he answers.

Together, we turn and look up to the Leland mansion far off on the hill. It's a cloudy day and the ground feels cold and hard and still. A shiver goes down my back. I don't even remember reaching out, but Briggs and I are holding hands.

Somewhere out there in the distance is the labyrinth. And Will.

Chapter 44

"C'mon," I say. "We have to hurry."

Briggs pauses. "Okay, but first, just stop and think for a second. What if he's already done? I mean, if you haven't heard from him, he could be on his way home."

I look up into Briggs's hopeful face and shake my head. "If he were done, we would have passed him on the way up. Plus, his bike is hidden behind the bushes and his stuff is here."

I show Briggs our phones behind the giant stone and

try to explain. "There's no service here anyway—and it's just something Will wants. It's—it's a Will thing. And I hated seeing his phone just lying alone there...." I feel a little silly.

Briggs nods and then adds his phone next to ours. And that little act and seeing our phones lined up there, side by side—like a family—like a secret club—it's just another thing I really like about Briggs.

"This way if we pass each other, he'll see our phones here and figure out we're here, too. He'll probably wait and then we'll all go home together."

Oh, I like the idea of this. And it could happen. It could. Briggs told me that Will has a routine for calming down, and the whole point of coming here to the labyrinth was because it's all Zen and relaxing. Maybe he's already walked through it and he's calm and we'll run into each other any minute now, and he's so Zen that he won't even lecture me the whole way home. I wanted to walk through it with him more than anything, but if Will would just show up right now, I'd be fine and would gladly take any lecture he had to offer instead.

"Maybe," I say. "It could happen."

Briggs buttons his peacoat. It's navy blue and looks like something a sailor would wear. It doesn't really go with his fedora. But it goes with him. "Okay, how far is it?"

I wish I had an exact answer. "From Will's research, we guess that it's about a twenty-minute walk if we go straight, keeping the mansion to our far right and over that hill, but we never got to practice this part. So we're not sure."

"How late are you?"

I cringe. "Late. Really late. And we've been standing here talking so long already and it gets dark early. We have to go."

We set off and try to keep up a fast pace, but the first part of the property is rough walking. The tree roots rise and fall, trying to trip us up. There are rocks everywhere, some rough and loose and others as big as boulders. We try to keep going straight, but the hills throw us off and we have to turn and change our direction a few times until all the roughness finally turns into Mr. Leland's beautiful manicured lawns.

The walk feels like much more than twenty minutes. No labyrinth or greenhouse in sight. How could we have calculated so wrong?

"How big is their land, anyway?" Briggs whispers as we start up the biggest hill yet.

I fill Briggs in on all our information as we climb. I tell him about Jenny Leland and choosing between Brandon and Gruber and Mr. Leland's hard silver hair. The Windy City masons and the Doggy Plaza.

"Wow. You know a lot. I didn't think anyone knew anything about the Lelands or the mansion. Like, it's always been this big mystery."

"Will has this thing...this thing about having as much information as you can to make the right decisions. Paying attention to details."

Something I haven't done at all.

Like now.

As we reach the top of the hill, I turn to look back down at the bottom. Because something is different up here. Something feels different. There's something wrong. What is it?

I look at Briggs and squint.

The light.

It's fading.

In a panic, I look overhead. Cloudy. Which means

no moon. Or stars. When the sun goes down, it will be pitch black. And that's going to be soon.

"What time is it? Do you have a watch?"

"No, but I have my pho—" Briggs freezes as he reaches for his pocket.

I try to calculate. What time did I leave the hospital? How long did I wait for Briggs? I promised Mom I'd be back before dark. She'll be worried. I don't even have a way to let her know I'm okay.

Or to find out if she and my baby sister are.

We have to keep moving. We have to find Will, so I can get back to my mom.

"I'll go get my phone," says Briggs. "I can sprint there and back and then at least we'll have a little light." He's still looking down the huge hill we just climbed.

"No!" I hold on to his arm. I turn and look about wildly, scanning the property. "Wait. From up here, we should be able to see it. I'm sure we're almost—the greenhouse!" I point. "Which means it should be just over ... there."

There, indeed.

Finally. In the distance.

The famous Leland Labyrinth.

I know it's made of green leafy hedges, but in the dying light, it's a castle of solid black. All sharp edges cutting into the air. How can it look so big when it's still so far away?

"That's not even a—a mile away. Is it?" Briggs asks.

"Less." Though it's hard to tell, because the air has that off-focus haze that happens right before the sun sets. "Maybe half a mile."

"But I should still run and get the phones," Briggs says. "I can meet you there."

I haven't let go of his arm. "But it's so close. Half a mile is two times around the track at school—ten blocks in the city. We should just go now, follow the path, find Will, and get out." I try to pull him forward and stumble because now it's getting so dark, I'm having trouble seeing the ground. "We can find our way back in the dark."

Briggs squeezes my arm.

"We will. Even if we reach the wrong part of the wall, we'll just follow it along until we find the opening again. Let's—"

"Shhhh!" Briggs is holding his finger to his mouth.

"Briggs—"

"Shhh!" He pulls me to the ground and I sit down hard.

"Ow! What's the—"

He points and I follow the line of his outstretched arm. And then I see it, too.

A flashlight.

Stabbing its way through the dark. As if searching.

Did we trip an alarm? Were there hidden cameras?

"But—but no one is supposed to be home! Jenny Leland said her uncle never changes his plans—never! And the Killer Hounds are at the—"

A howl cuts me off as the last of the sunlight fades and the evening goes dark.

Sometimes plans change.

Chapter 45

We jump to our feet, already breathing hard as if we've been running for miles. For a split second, we can only stare at the bobbing flashlight, now bobbing faster and faster as if it's picked up speed. Another howl snaps us out of it.

"RUN!" Briggs yells, and we sprint as hard as we can for the labyrinth.

Just get there before the hounds!

Just get there before the hounds!

Am I shouting the words to Briggs in the dark? Or

is he shouting them to me? Or maybe it's just my feet against the cold, hard ground pounding the words into my brain.

Get there before the hounds?

And then what?

Won't they come in right after us? Chasing us down through the turns until we fall?

I twist my head around to see if they're gaining on us and my foot hits something—a rock, a root, it doesn't matter. I go flying forward and skid into the ground, my hands hitting first. I crumple into a roll and stop. I try to push myself up, but I'm dizzy and my hands hurt.

I hear Briggs's voice from somewhere above. "Bea!"

Something heavy lands on top of me and I realize it's him. Briggs is huddled over me—shielding me as the sound of running feet and jangling chains closes in on us.

"Call them off! We're just kids!" he yells, and squeezes his arms around me in protection. "Call them off!"

I brace myself.

Then nothing.

Jangle. Jangle.

"Sit, Petunia!" a voice says. "Good boy."

That voice. I know that voice.

I'd know it anywhere. I've been listening to it for most of my life. Though it hasn't spoken directly to me since the pool party on the last Saturday before school began.

Chapter 46

Sometimes in the middle of the craziest moments in your life, you hear yourself say the most ridiculous thing.

"You... got a dog."

I manage to raise myself out of the tangle of arms and legs that Briggs and I have become, and there she is.

S is standing in front of me. Shining a flashlight in my face. Looking directly at me for the first time this year. A silence grows in the space between us, and I know we're both thinking about how we used to say we were going to get a pet together. S wanted a dog, but I was afraid of them and wanted a cat. I finally said I'd take a dog, but only a really small dog. She wanted a big one. Petunia is medium. The kind that looks like a fox with eyeliner and a curly tail.

"Yeah."

"A boy—named Petunia?"

"Yeah."

Yeah and *Yeah*. The only words she's said to me so far all school year.

I want to ask her a million questions. But nothing comes out. I scramble up and busy myself checking my backpack.

"How did you—" I begin.

"I—I overheard you talking about going to the maze thing that day at our—at the Wall. It sounded important. And then, today, your dad said you were biking on the Neck with us."

I can feel my face heating up. "It's a labyrinth—and I wasn't trying to bike with you. I only said that because I needed an excuse—"

"I know," she says. "I figured it out. I just wanted to help." She shines the flashlight on me again and sees that my arms are now crossed. "I told the—I told them I had to go...."

"We have to go, too," I say, slipping my backpack back on.

Briggs has gotten up from the ground. "You're Jay's sister, aren't you?"

Of course. He remembers her from the pool party.

My mouth works to form a name I haven't said out loud in almost three months.

"Briggs. This is... Sammie."

"She should come," Briggs says. "She's the only one smart enough to bring a flashlight."

"I don't care," I manage to say. "I just want to find Will."

"Hey, Petunia." Briggs holds a hand out and Petunia licks him. "Why was she—I mean *he* howling like that?"

S is shivering. She jumps up and down. "I don't know. He never barks unless something really terrible's happening."

I'm glad for the dark because I still can't quite look at her. Hasn't something terrible been happening all year?

271

"Can we go?" I say.

"Sure," Briggs says. "Sammie, why don't you hold on to Petunia and I'll hold the flashlight."

I see it clearly as Sammie hands it to him. It's pink plastic with a rainbow sticker on it. From my birthday sleepover party in fourth grade.

Sammie sees me looking. "I—I just grabbed it. It's the first one I saw."

Briggs clicks it on and off a few times. "Okay, so we're sure Will is somewhere in there."

I nod. "He's in there."

"Do you think he's hurt?" Sammie asks.

"Hurt?" I haven't even thought about him being hurt. Just wandering around, cold and scared. "I hope he's not. I hope he's just walking and being...calm."

Briggs nods.

And the way Sammie nods, I can tell she's heard the story. Even though Mrs. Reegs asked everyone to stay quiet about it, I guess people are going to talk.

"Let's just go in," I say. "The path will take us to the center and then back out the same way. It'll turn and wind a lot, but no matter what, we'll run into Will sooner or later."

272

I grip the straps of my backpack tightly and think of the jacket inside. I'm going to reach Will. I'm going to make sure he's warm and safe.

"Ready?" Briggs says.

"Ready," I answer.

"Ready," Sammie echoes, and we cross the last stretch of grass to the labyrinth and walk under the arch that, until today, no one outside the Leland family has been through in over fifty years.

Chapter 47

The arch looms over us, tripled in size with the dark. We hesitate for a moment. Then I take a step forward and Briggs and Sammie follow me.

We're in.

We walk in tight formation. At one point, I see Sammie staring down at Briggs and me holding hands, but I don't care what she thinks, I'm not letting go. I squeeze his hand tighter. He squeezes back.

Will. He's here. He has to be. We saw his bike. We

walked directly to the labyrinth. There's no way we could have missed each other if he was heading back home. Is there? We did get a little lost—no. Will's here. Somewhere in the dark and there's only one way to find him.

Follow the path.

It takes an immediate right and goes straight for a distance. Then a hairpin turn in the opposite direction. Another long straight path and another hairpin turn. Straight and turn. Straight and turn. Just like the drawings that Will does, it will go on like this till we reach the center. I try to imagine it in the daylight the way Will wanted to see it, surrounded with beautiful, calming green, but in the dark . . . I shiver.

We're cautious at first. Walking slowly. The thin beam of the flashlight steadily moves back and forth as Briggs carefully searches every inch of the path. We fall into a rhythm. Straight and turn. Then I notice he's keeping the light angled down on the ground. Briggs thinks—he thinks that when we find Will, he'll be—

I pick up the pace.

Straight and turn.

Will's not huddled on the ground somewhere. He's

not. But every shadow that appears makes me rush forward. Every bump in the grass makes me stop.

I walk fast. And then faster.

Straight and turn.

Will is smart. He knows how to figure things out. He knows how to calm himself down. Just because it's dark, it doesn't mean—

Straight and turn.

We go even faster. We just have to get to him. We just—

The path splits.

No one moves for a moment. Briggs shines the light one way and then the other. "But—but I thought there was only one path up and back."

"There is. There aren't supposed to be any choices. You just...go through." I try to remember if Will has ever told me about a different kind of labyrinth. But he hasn't. I know he hasn't. "Let's just head down the right side a little," I say.

"Are you sure?" asks Sammie.

I don't answer. Because I'm not. Of course I'm not.

I just go. And they follow.

"Slow down," Briggs says.

I don't.

I go faster. Briggs and Sammie don't say anything else. They just keep up.

The flashlight becomes shaky and frantic, darting from one tall hedge to the next, but no matter how fast we go or how far the light shines, it's all the same: Will is nowhere.

And then we turn another corner and—

Face a solid wall.

Briggs spins around. "I thought you said—" He slashes the light up and down and across the hedge as if he could cut his way through. "What's going on?"

Sammie gives a frightened little whisper. "What is it?"

I open my mouth.

"It's…a blind alley," I answer.

"But how do we—how do we get back to the one-path part? Bea?"

A labyrinth is a single path.
A labyrinth is a single path.
A labyrinth is a single path.

"A labyrinth is a single path," I say.

Briggs moves close to me. His voice is low. "What does it mean?"

"It means that...Leland Labyrinth is not a labyrinth," I say.

"What is it?" whispers Briggs.

But I think he already knows the answer.

"It's a maze."

Chapter 48

Sammie starts fumbling with her phone. "We need to call for help! We need to get someone here." She shakes her old flip phone and then looks up at us. "Try your phones! Mine's not working—is yours?"

I shake my head.

Briggs looks like he's going to be sick. "We don't have them, but even if we did, there's no cell reception here."

Sammie is holding her phone up in the air and swinging it around. "Are you sure? Then we have to go back, right? We didn't take that many turns. Did we? We can't be that lost!"

"We can't leave," I say. "Will is in here—"

Will is in here.

Will is in Leland Labyrinth, but it's not a Zen place with a Zen center and one path. It's not a perfect masterpiece. There are no safe places here. And I don't know what to do.

I turn to Briggs. "Please. Fix this."

"Wh-what?"

"Fix this. You're the one who fixes things. You fixed the antiques at the *Broadside* office. You fixed the typewriter—"

"The typewriter..." says Briggs.

I stumble. I didn't mean to bring up the notes or him liking me at a time like this.

"Plus—you're the oldest." I know how lame this sounds.

"But you know more. You know all about mazes and the Lelands and this—this stuff!"

I look at Briggs, and then at Sammie, who is still waving her phone. Someone needs to take charge.

"Fine..." I say. "Well—" I stop and then start again.

"Well, first of all, we are not leaving." I glare at them and no one fights me on this. "But we still need to find our way out for *after* we find Will. So we need something— something to keep track of our path so we can get out again. Like bread crumbs, but better..." I have nothing on me but two thermoses of hot chocolate. Could I pour them to leave a trail?

Sammie speaks up. "Wait... I think I..." I can hear her searching her shoulder bag. She pulls something out. "Will this work?"

Briggs shines the flashlight on her and it's a ball of pink yarn. It's attached to a crochet hook and there is about a two-foot piece of zigzag pattern hanging from it.

"You carry that around with you?" I ask.

Sammie nods. She knows what I'm thinking. I have a green ball of yarn at home. Right before I left for Taiwan, we started them. Mine was zigzag green and blue. Sammie's was zigzag pink and orange. We were going to make crochet blankets together. "I still want to make it," she says. "I mean, I still want to work on it, but I don't even know if there's enough here...."

Briggs grabs it. "It'll work...." He pulls off the crochet hook and holds on to the yarn hanging off the end, handing me the ball. "Hold this." He takes the flashlight with him and disappears back the way we came. Sammie and I wait there in the dark. I hold the ball loosely in my cupped hands, feeling it jump and spin. I picture the zigzag blanket that we wanted so badly to make, unraveling tiny bump by bump as Briggs moves farther and farther away from us, back to the entrance. It finally stops. Sammie and I don't speak. It feels like hours before he's back.

Is he okay?

Does he remember which way we turned after the split?

Was it right or left? I can't think.

Finally, we hear him coming back and he arrives, out of breath.

"Okay, we're still pretty close to the beginning. I tied the end to a branch at the entrance so we'll be able to find our way back—" He looks at me. "After we find Will."

He holds a hand out to me and I take it as we leave the blind alley and walk farther into the maze. I try not to think about how he didn't say if he thinks the yarn is long enough.

Chapter 49

The third-biggest labyrinth in the country feels like the longest one in the world. As we walk, I try to figure things out.

But nothing makes sense.

Will researched and researched everything he could about the Lelands. He was so sure. And Will is never wrong.

How could he be so wrong?

Briggs and Sammie let me take the lead. I choose left or right without thinking and keep us moving forward.

I do not have a plan. All thoughts of having a plan disappeared at that first dead end. Sammie and I do not speak. She takes turns holding Petunia and letting him trot beside her. Petunia chews on Sammie's jeans. He runs forward to me and nips at my ankles.

"Ow!" I yelp. "She—he bit me!"

"Sorry," Sammie says. "I'm really sorry. He can't help himself."

"That's okay. It didn't hurt," I say. But when I see how relieved she is, I get angry. "Actually, it really did hurt—I mean really, really hurt. You can't just—just do that, you know. Let your—let Petunia hurt people, I mean."

Sammie doesn't answer.

We walk in silence.

Every minute or so, Briggs whisper-shouts, "Will!"

We keep checking that Sammie's pink yarn does not break or tear. It's our only way out.

"Did you double-knot it on the hedge?" I ask Briggs.

"Yes...no. I don't know," he answers.

"You did. I'm sure you did."

If it's possible, it actually feels as if it's getting even darker.

"Briggs, can you shine the flashlight ahead? I can't see." Petunia nips at my jeans again. "Ow, cut it out—Briggs, what's wrong?"

He's stopped walking and the yarn pulls tight between us. He's hitting the flashlight against the palm of his hand. And it's flickering.

"What's—" Sammie begins, but she doesn't have to say any more, we all see it. The flashlight is fading.

I turn to her. "Are you kidding? You couldn't check the batteries?"

"I was in a rush. I haven't used it since—"

"Ha! Fourth-grade sleepover," I say. "I know—I gave it to you!"

"At least I brought a flashlight!" Sammie says. "Do you have a light? Do you have *anything* to offer? Oh, I know—how about a *poem*?" She mimics wild writing in the air.

"Stop," Briggs says.

But she doesn't. And the way she acts it out with her arms jerking and waving. So angry. So angry at me for being...me.

I don't know where to look. I stare into the last bit of light from the flashlight as it fades till it looks like a torch with the tiniest flame. Then I remember something. I slip off my backpack, unzip the little section I never use, and pull out the pack of matches.

"I have...this," I say.

My invisible ink matches. I hid them away in here the day I found out that Briggs was the one I had been writing to. I pull out my stack of three-by-three-inch squares.

"And paper."

I hold it up.

There's barely any light from the flashlight now, but it's enough for Briggs to see how small the papers are. "How fast will those burn up?" he asks.

"I don't know."

"So what do we do? Make a torch?"

"What if we...we can try to space them out." I hold up one square. "I'll light the match to just one page and then we can see how long it lasts and...what we see."

No one says anything.

Sammie puts away her phone.

It's not the best plan, but no one else has anything to offer.

"Okay. So..." I resettle my backpack on my back, hearing the thermoses clink against each other. Then I pick up one page and hand the rest to Briggs.

Zzzzffft!

I strike the match and quickly hold it to the edge of the first piece of paper. As it catches, I realize I'm holding it at the top and lighting from the bottom, and the flames are heading straight for my fingers, and just as I let out a little yell,

act the way—

Words appear on the page and I drop it.

Invisible ink from the day I was trying to write the "Act the Way I Wish I Were" haiku. I wrote those words out over and over again, wishing and wondering what it would be like if I could just change. Change from the person Sammie walked away from. And now here is a whole stack of those words for Briggs and Sammie to see.

They are stomping the little flame into the ground.

"Sorry," I manage to say.

"Don't be. Do you want me to do it?" asks Briggs.

"No. No, I got it." I shake my head. It doesn't matter what they see. Finding Will is the only important thing. I take a deep breath. "What if we leave as much slack as we can in the yarn and as soon as I light the paper, I yell *go* and we just—just run as far as we can?"

No one answers.

I answer myself, "Okay, then...here we go." I get another match. "Ready?"

Zzzzffft!

wish I

The flame lasts no longer than the first line of a haiku...*one...two...three...four...five...*

And in that time, I take in whatever I can. Hedges! Path! Shadows! Up ahead—a right turn!

"Go! Straight and right!" I shout. And we stumble along until the light dies. I drop the last bit before it burns my fingers, and we stomp and stomp it into the ground.

Again and again, we do this.

Zzzzffft!

still act—

Zzzzffft!

if I

Zzzzffft!

or be—

Words blooming and wilting as I burn page after page.

wish
acting or

becoming

wish

if

if

am I

And in the *one...two...three...four...five* between rushing forward and stomping out the ashes, I think about how when these words burn up and fly feather-light into the air, there will be no more chances for anyone else to see them. They will only ever exist in this moment, during this time, when I am running and Will is lost.

I don't know if we've been in here for five minutes or five hours or five years.

As I'm waiting for Briggs to hand me the next piece of paper, there's a long pause before he says, "This is the last one."

I don't answer right away. "This is the last match...."

"What do we do now?" Sammie whispers.

"We have to be close, right?" asks Briggs. "How big can this thing be?"

The third biggest in the country. "We—we've gotten pretty far," I say. "I think—stop it, Petunia! Sammie, can you please—"

"Petunia! Bad boy—come here!" I hear scuffling and jangling. "Do you have him?"

"No."

"He's—quick! Grab his—follow him!"

Follow him? The three of us stumble in the dark in the direction of Petunia's jangling run. I think I hear Briggs crash into a hedge and scramble out.

"Where is he? Do you hear him?" Sammie cries. "Petunia!"

We stand still for a moment and listen.

Nothing, but silence.

Then an outburst of panicked barking.

"Something's wrong!" Sammie cries. "Petunia never barks—Beezy, light the match! Light the match! Please!"

It's the last one, but I do it anyway and I don't know if it's because of how scared Sammie sounds or because of the name she hasn't used since kindergarten.

But I do it.

Zzzzffft!

Sometimes things happen so fast, your brain can only comprehend them in slow motion. And as I try to understand the scenes that rise and fade before me in the flickering light, the pounding of my heart echoes in my ears, counting down the seconds like an underwater drum—

five ... dead end

four ... Petunia barking

three ... there's someone—

two . . . "It's Will! It's—"

. . . one.

I see it in the instant before everything goes black.

A shape in the dark.

Crouched, ready to leap. Snarling mouth. Ears flattened back. Standing over Will. *Standing over Will.* And something inside me builds so big and so fast, I know it can't be stopped. Not by walls or words or whatever weakness Will says I have. Because it's stronger than all those things, and it will not let anyone or anything hurt my friend.

"NO! YOU LEAVE HIM ALONE—I AM NOT AFRAID OF YOU!"

And I don't think

I just do—

I charge forward, swinging my backpack high above my head and bringing it down as hard as I can.

Chapter 50

GONG!

I scream.

Briggs and Sammie are shouting somewhere behind me in the dark.

"Bea!"

"Will!"

"Where are you?"

"What happened?"

I've fallen and tumbled somewhere between gravel and grass, and I'm crawling on the ground, feeling my way to Will. I'm not sure why I don't have fangs stuck in my back. Or what that sound like a hollow drum was.

I reach out and my fingers feel something soft—a T-shirt!

"Will!"

I grab his shoulders. He's freezing. "B-b-bea—"

"You guys! Here! Help me!"

Petunia is still barking and jumping up and down, nipping at my ankles.

I see the faint light of Sammie's phone bobbing toward us.

Briggs crawls over to us. "Will, are you okay?"

I have one hand holding on to Will and the other trying to find my backpack when my arm hits something cold and solid. Like a table leg. No. A hound leg. But metal. I feel my way around.

"It's—it's a statue—the hound is a statue," I say.

"What do you mean?" says Briggs. "The Killer Hounds? They're all statues?"

"This one is! I don't know." I knock on it three times. *Gong! Gong! Gong!* "But never mind that. Please, help me find my backpack; I have a jacket for Will in there."

Will tries to say something again, but he's shaking

too hard, and I don't know what to do. I try rubbing warmth back into his arms, while Briggs pats his way along the grass in the dark. I finally hear the sound of a zipper, and a soft jacket lands on me. It's soaked and smells sickly sweet. The hot chocolate. It's spilled and leaked everywhere. Before I can say a word, Briggs whips off his peacoat and hands it to me, and if I had more than a second to think, I know that this would be added to the list of things I like about Briggs. The things I like so very, very much. His coat is still warm inside. I try to get Will into it as fast as I can.

"Will, are you okay?" I say. "I'm so, so sorry I'm late. I'm going to get you warm—I just need to—argh—" I struggle with the stiff wool. "Briggs—these buttons are impossible!" I finally manage them and flip the collar up so it covers Will's neck.

Will opens his mouth. "T-t-t—"

"What's the matter? Are you hurt?"

"T-tag."

"Tag?" I burst out in something between a laugh and a cry. "Oh, Will. I know. I'm so sorry, but it's the only coat we have. How long have you been lying here?"

"D-don't know," he answers. "You w-weren't inside

the wall, b-but you're never late. Then I remembered you wanted to change the plan—even though I said not to. But maybe I didn't repeat it enough times to you. You d-don't really get things unless they're repeated a lot."

I nod. It's true. I'm the girl who needs things repeated. I need to listen more.

"You said to meet just inside the labyrinth. B-but then you weren't there and I didn't know if you'd changed the plan more and were just ahead of me. And then..."

"It wasn't a labyrinth anymore," I finish. "It doesn't matter. Let's get you out of here. Briggs, the yarn!"

"Got it. I just have to..." I hear him reeling it in. Pulling till it gets tight, so we can follow it back. "It's stuck on someth—"

Petunia suddenly yelps.

"Oh no..." Sammie's voice carries over to us.

"What's wrong? What happened?" Briggs asks.

"I'm sorry," Sammie says. "Petunia's—he's all tangled up in it. He must have..."

Everything goes quiet.

"You—you can get us out of here, right?" Will asks.

No one says anything.

Petunia howls.

And this time, I know it's not a Killer Hound, but it still sends a chill straight through me. We have no light. The night is dark and endless and cold and we are lost in the third-largest *maze* in the country—

"Bea?"

I don't answer. My hand is clutching my chest and I am counting out the beats of words I don't want to say.

I do not know the way

(six)

Chapter 51

We have pulled ourselves into a tight circle on the ground. Sammie holds on to Petunia, her phone giving no more light than a firefly. Briggs is shaking in the wet jacket he tried to wring dry.

"Ohh-k-kay," says Briggs. His voice is quivery. "To sum up: n-no yarn. No cell service. Anyone else?"

"We can't wait till morning. My mom will freak out," Sammie says.

I don't even want to think about my mom yet. How

she doesn't know where I am. How I don't even know if I have a little sister yet. Or if she and my mom are okay.

"Will?" I ask. "Maybe there's something about mazes, you know—"

Will shakes his head. "I told you, I don't like mazes. I like them even less now. This was supposed to be a labyrinth. It was supposed to be a geometric masterpiece. It was supposed to be—"

"I know, I know." I bury my face in my hands.

Perfect. Why is everyone so obsessed with everything being perfect? Mrs. Reegs said she gave me the perfect novel. Jenny Leland said my mom made perfect art. Even stupid Dan Ross...

Stupid, braggy Dan Ross.

I rise to my feet. "Will..."

"Yes."

"You thought this labyrinth would be...perfect."

"Well, it's not."

I turn around in a slow circle. It's dark and I can't see it, but I know that the blind alley is in front of me. "But what if...what if it is?"

"What are you talking about?" asks Sammie.

"Remember what Mr. Clarke said in class?" I say. "The Extra Credit Curveball."

Sammie is the only one in that class with me. "About *The Karate Kid*?"

"No, the other—" I shake my head. "Will."

"Yes."

"The best way to figure out what to do is to look at all the information you have, right?"

"Yes."

When I close my eyes, I can see things more clearly.

I can see all the walls of Dan Ross's maze just as I did that day on my tiptoes. Mr. Clarke told us that it was a perfect maze and that a perfect maze can be solved. But what makes something perfect? What did Mrs. Reegs say about the novel she gave me? What did Jenny Leland say about my mom's art? How do I feel when a poem is...just right?

My hand makes its way over my heart.

Bah-bump.

I open my eyes. It's still pitch black out, but I see. I see everything.

"It's connected," I say.

"What is?" asks Briggs.

"The walls. The maze. Everything. Everything is connected!" I turn to Will. "Pick a wall." My heart has started beating fast and my voice is shaking.

"What do you mean?"

"Pick a wall, Will. What if this is a perfect maze? Like the one you got for your birthday and didn't like." I close my eyes again. "And if it is...if we could look down on it right now, we'd see that all the walls are connected. Connected and holding each other up. Which means, everything in here is connected and—"

"There's a routine to get out." Will's voice sounds stronger.

"There's a routine to get out," I repeat. "You put your hand on a wall. Don't let go and keep moving forward."

Will nods. "If all the walls of the maze are connected to each other, it means they're also connected to the exit. So if we keep walking the maze, always touching the wall with our same hands, always going the same way, we'll eventually reach the exit. And get out."

"But are you sure?" whispers Sammie. "That this is the same kind of maze? As...as Dan's?"

I pause before I answer. "...No."

We form a line without speaking, and each put our

right hand on the wall and our left hand on the shoulder of the person in front of us.

Me first. Will next. Then Sammie. And Briggs.

I'm shaking, but I raise my chin and stare into the dark.

I don't know if this is the same kind of maze. I don't know what's ahead or if I'm making the right choice. The only thing I do know is that I'm afraid—and I'm still going to try anyway. The weight of Will's hand presses into my shoulder and I know something else. No matter what happens next, I have someone behind me.

Chapter 52

I lead us out.

We exit the maze and find the property bathed in moonlight. The clouds have moved on, and we can see our way back up to the broken part of the wall.

I peek back at Sammie and I wonder what will happen tomorrow at school. But then I guess you never really know what happens next. You can only do the best you can while you're in the moment.

When we reach the part of the park where we can

get cell service, Sammie calls her mom, and she drives over in minutes.

She gets teary when she sees me and hugs me close. Then she laughs and hugs Will and Briggs, too.

"You're safe and you're here and you all look so tired right now, I'm not even going to ask. But I called every one of your parents, and you can explain it to them. I don't know what you're doing in a park at night when it closes at sunset, but I get it." She smiles at us and the way she walks back to the car, it's like I can hear her theme song playing.

When we get to Will's house, he says something to Briggs that I can't hear. But I see Briggs nod and pat his shoulder. Then Will turns to me and says, "I know it's important for you to know that I appreciate you. So, THANK YOU for saving me."

"Well, I made up a list of all the information, and you, Will, are totally worth saving."

"You are, too," he answers.

I laugh. Then stop when I see how serious he looks.

"See you at school tomorrow," I say.

"Yes," he answers.

Briggs grins at me before he gets out at his house. And tips his hat. "Standing-ovation-worthy evening," he says, in a way that makes me remember something.

"That day...at the pool party..." I can feel S not moving, next to me. "Did you—you were the one who clapped for me, weren't you?"

Briggs just keeps grinning as he steps out of the car and waves.

When we finally get to the hospital, it's like I'm looking at two different Sammies. There's the Sammie who hasn't spoken to me since the last weekend before school. And there's the one who came to the Leland estate to help. She had yarn and a flashlight from our fourth-grade sleepover and a medium-sized dog. We argued. But we also found Will. And we got out.

She opens her mouth, but before I know which

Sammie is going to speak, her mom says, "When I called your parents to let them know I have you, they said you have to hurry and meet your little sister!"

So neither Sammie ends up saying anything.

But then neither do I.

I thank her mom and run inside.

Before I go to my mom's room, I stop at the nurses' station and see a nurse at each end of this big counter. I look back and forth between the two and then finally choose the woman nurse with the big smile instead of the man with the frown and ask, "Could I borrow a piece of paper and a blue pen, please?"

She looks around. "I have paper, but only a black pen."

And then the crabby-looking nurse says, "I have a blue one!" He holds it up and it's one of those terrible, lumpy ballpoint pens with no soul.

But I take it and say, "Thank you. It's perfect." Because it's here, right now in this hospital where my mom and my dad and my baby sister are waiting, and I have a blank page in front of me, so anything is possible.

And I've chosen a middle name.

Then I'm in the room and hugging my mom and she's all sleepy and pretty, and I can't stop laughing, because

Starling has so much hair and it's sticking straight up in the air like a black flame and her face is as round as a little Buddha, and both Mom and Dad swear that I had even more hair when I was born and my face was even rounder. I hand them the piece of paper, and what's written on it is not in indigo ink and speckled with stars as I had once imagined, but it's exactly what I want to give them right now.

They read quietly for a moment, then start crying. That is, Mom has a single sparkling tear on her perfectly smooth cheek. And Dad is making noises like a little kid and has to take off his glasses to mop up his eyes.

Mom turns to me. "I think it's exactly what I would have picked if I had thought of it, Trix. It's..." She places a hand over her heart, and our eyes meet.

bah-bump, bah-bump

"Starling." Mom kisses the top of my baby sister's head. "You have a middle name."

I kiss her, too, and whisper, "I hope you like it... Starling Blue."

I look into my mom's face, and it's like we're back in

her studio and her painting is bigger than the sky and she is floating in a world filled with shooting stars and jeweled birds; only this time, I am floating with her.

...I love the blue, too...

"And you...and you," Mom whispers into my hair. She holds me as close as she can with my baby sister between us. "Do you have any idea how much I love you, Trix?"

I nod into her shoulder.

I do...I do...

Chapter 53

I t is Monday and I am on the path.

I am by the Wall.

I am waiting.

But it's a different kind of waiting.

It's the kind of waiting where you think maybe you're not going to wait anymore. It's not too late yet. If I leave now, I'll actually get to class early. So I think that's what I'm going to do.

I walk the rest of the way to school and it's funny....

This is the same path that I know so well, that I've walked hundreds of times, but today, all I can think is that the more you walk down a path, the more you start to feel that you can probably handle whatever it is you find at the end.

Chapter 54

In the hallway, I see Mrs. Reegs laughing with Mr. Clarke and she doesn't look like stumbling, awkward, thumbs-up Mrs. Reegs. She looks almost like she does when...when she talks to us kids. Her sneakers have bright-yellow happy faces on them.

"Hi, Mrs. Reegs! Hi, Mr. Clarke!" I call out. They wave and come over.

"Good morning, Bea!" Mrs. Reegs says. "How are you? How's the book?"

"I finished it," I say. Actually, before I went to the

Leland estate. But now, it feels as if I finished it a million years ago.

"You did." She smiles. "And?"

"Well, you said this was a book about 'being,' right?"

Mrs. Reegs nods.

"Well, at first, she was being herself. But then that sort of caused some problems. Mostly for people who didn't even matter. Then she was acting like someone else. And that made this one person who *did* matter really happy. But *she* wasn't happy."

"And now?" asks Mrs. Reegs.

"And now, I think she's just..." I grasp around for words. Then it hits me and I look up at her. "It's like she finally made a decision that even though it might mean that she won't be around this one person anymore, she wants to go back to just..." I look up at her and smile. "Just...you know."

Mrs. Reegs nods. She knows.

"But I kind of can't stop thinking about the narrator."

"What about the narrator?"

"It's too bad that person couldn't stand by her and be there for her. Especially because I think they really regretted it." I blink back sudden tears. "I think sometimes people are just scared and feel all this pressure and don't know what to do. But I also don't think being scared should stop you from something—big and important."

Mrs. Reegs nods again. "Good book, huh?"

I sigh. "It's pretty much perfect."

I clear my throat and turn to Mr. Clarke. "Speaking of perfect, I did it, by the way."

"Excellent!" He gives me a big handshake. The kind they do in cartoons where they pump their hands way up and down three times. "Never doubted you would! Not for a nanosecond. Just tell me this: What did you do?"

"I solved the perfect maze," I say. "For the Extra. Credit. Curveball." I make sure to pronounce each word precisely so it sinks in, and then I laugh as Mr. Clarke's mouth drops open. "You know it actually did exactly what you said." As I'm speaking, I realize it's true. "Figuring out the Extra Credit Curveball also helped me figure out this huge thing that was going on in my life. It made—it really made a difference."

Mr. Clarke stammers a little. "D-did it?" He starts fumbling with his books. No one has ever done one of his Extra Credit Curveballs before. He looks at me and in a soft voice says, "Thank you, Beatrix. As a teacher, you try to find a way to connect, but..." Wait. Are his eyes all watery? Grown-ups are so weird.

I notice that he's shaved off his very last bit of facial hair, which was a pencil mustache last week. "Hey," I say, pointing to his face. "I like it. This is my favorite."

Mr. Clarke suddenly looks like his old joking self again. "Well, thank you, young lady. So. This is an Extra Credit Curveball first. What should we do? Maybe have it all written up and professionally bound? Or..." He looks at me. Like maybe he's figured out something new about me. "You might consider presenting it to the class?"

I look at him a moment.

And nod.

"Well, that would be a thing to behold, Miss Beatrix...*Bruce?* Lee," he tries.

I laugh. "You know, Mr. Clarke, I don't even have a middle name."

"No middle name! What foul sorcery is this? How will I go on? Where will I find joy?" He shakes his fist to the sky, then stops and smiles at me. "So...just Beatrix Lee?"

"My parents always said it was enough. I used to be

314

pretty mad about it when I was little, so they let me pick my baby sister's middle name. She was born last night and her name is Starling Blue."

Mr. Clarke winks at me. Grown-ups do things like that. Wink. I guess they think it makes them seem like they're in on it with you or something. But I think it just makes him seem . . . like him.

"Well, congratulations on being a big sister. Now, if you will excuse me, I am going to walk Ms. Rodriguez to the teachers' lounge to replenish her caffeine stock. Plus, there's a meeting of fellow teachers to discuss how someone is trying to change our softball league to croquet—which I shall fight to the death! See you in class, Just Bea."

Mrs. Reegs gives me a Look and a wave as they walk off, and I think about how I like that her Look today isn't about anything except being happy that she's heading to a gathering of friends.

Chapter 55

When I get to Social Studies Colon Ancient Civilizations, I pause outside the door and peek in. I'm early. Sammie and Lisa and Lizbeth and Allegra are in the far corner with Dan Ross and a few other boys.

I go to my regular seat like always. I slide my backpack neatly under like always.

Sammie doesn't move. She doesn't say a word.

And the way she is frozen there, standing so still, makes me wish I could put a golden-nibbed pen or even a bumpy blue ballpoint into her hand and lead her to the nearest wall.

Or hand her a blue book with a yellow stick figure.

Or find a theme song to make her want to sing in the street.

Like this one song on the *I Hope You Listen* playlist. A song I picked because I wanted to tell her she doesn't have to stand there so still and afraid and hand-twisty, because it's not worth it to be with people who make you feel like you can't say what you want to say. Or be the way you want to be.

And I think about this.

And I am still thinking as I'm about to slide my headphones off...but

I keep them on, and

for the first time since this summer,

I take the wire out of my pocket and

plug it into my phone

and I hit Play and I haven't heard it in forever, but the minute it begins,

I remember that it starts with

a heartbeat.

buum-bah bah-dum-dum

317

buum-bah dah-dum

And I can feel my own heart as I close my eyes and think about how this entire playlist has always been a message I wanted to send to Sammie to say so many things.

I look at the label I made.

I Hope You Listen.

I look at it

and I think about something Will said about messages and how you have to decide who you are going to send them to—because messages need to be heard—

and then I turn the song up

and

I sit back

and

I listen.

Mr. Clarke won't mind. We have a few minutes until he gets here and class begins, and I'll just tell him this is my way of getting ready to do my perfect maze presentation.

Chapter 56

Will looks up at me eating my egg boats. "If you had told me all the information, I could have figured out that Leland Labyrinth was not unicursal."

"I gave you serious information! I am like the Queen of Information. You never would have gotten near that labyrinth without me! Who found out about the broken wall? And the masons? And—oh, what was that one last little part: How to Get Out?" I smile and pop another egg boat into my mouth.

"We never would have gone and gotten lost in the

first place if I had known everything. So, I've made a list of all the information that you did NOT give me—"

"Will, you're joking."

He looks at his list. "No."

"I was just—"

"ONE. The very first thing Jenny Leland told you was that Mr. Leland liked problem-solving. PROBLEM-SOLVING relaxes him—a PROBLEM—that's exactly what a multicursal maze is."

"But how was I supposed to—"

"TWO. The masons he had coming were GREEK. Kanakaris Masonry—he had plans to tear down the hedges and rebuild it in ancient Greek stone. ANCIENT GREEK STONE."

"What does that have to do with—"

"It further shows his obsession with Greece, and I would have known that his use of the word *labyrinth* was the original use and not the modern use. Do I have to repeat the difference to you again? The colloquial meaning—"

"I know! I know! But I definitely said 'Greek mason,' like, eighteen times during my conversation with Jenny

Leland. You were there! The whole conversation was Ancient Greek This, Ancient Greek That. It's not my fault you weren't listening."

"You know I'm an excellent listener," Will says. "And you did not say Greek mason once. Not once. You kept saying Windy City. Windy City masons. You did not tell me they were Greek masons or that Mr. Leland wanted ancient stones."

Oh yeah.

windy city

"I guess I just really like the way it sounds. I kept thinking I could write a poem—"

"THREE. If I knew that—"

"Will!"

"Yes."

"I'll do better next time."

"What next time?"

"Well, we still have to find a labyrinth for you, don't we?"

"...Yes."

I don't wait for him to ask me, and I am not even worried about what he'll say when I ask, "Can I help you?"

"Do you already know of another one? Did you research it? Is it close? This time you have to give me all the information. You'll write it down in a list."

"I will. I promise and—"

"Don't leave anything out this time."

"I won't, but Will, can you please stop interrupting me all the—"

"I don't interr—oh." He shuffles through his folder of papers and I know what he's looking for. A list. Where he can add another piece of information.

"And Will?"

"Yes."

"I brought you something."

I push a thermos toward him.

"What is it?"

"Hot chocolate."

"Why would you bring this when you know I always—"

Seriously?

"Because, Will," I say. "Because...it's important to let people know that you appreciate them...because I just

322

really, really want to say thank you, and because ... you're my friend." My throat suddenly catches. "I feel like ... like you're a friend who can't see you're there for me. And I don't know if I can ever make you see how much you mean...."

Will is quiet for a moment. He doesn't touch the thermos, but he raises his head and looks me in the face. Funny. I never realized he had gray eyes. He looks down again and softly says, "It doesn't have marshmallows, does it? I don't like the—what?"

When I'm finally done laughing, I tell him no, of course it doesn't.

Chapter 57

I think I get why Will likes lists so much.

I have a pretty long list of what I like about Briggs. And now I have something else to add: it looks like there isn't going to have to be a whole huge conversation about what happened at the labyrinth. Or the accidental hand-holding or the riding double or anything. We're just two people who... went through stuff together that doesn't need to be explained. I don't have to worry about what he thinks or feels about it. It's all right there. On his sleeve.

When I see Briggs in the *Broadside* office, I walk straight up to him and say, "So you know how I said I wasn't going to write poetry for the paper?"

He looks hopeful. "Ye-e-e-s?"

"Well...maybe I will....Do you like haiku?" I already know the answer.

"I do. A lot."

"I do, too...but I was thinking of doing something that's kind of a haiku, but also kind of...something all its own. Like if you tried to start a haiku, but then it didn't really work out, you could turn it into something else. Do you know what I mean?"

Briggs nods. "I think it should be whatever you want it to be."

I think so, too.

"When can I see it?"

"You'll be the first to know when and where," I say.

Briggs doesn't answer, he just pushes his fedora up so that I can see every inch of his smiling face.

That afternoon, I put a note inside the Portal.

> Hi.
> It's me and I know you know.
> And I know it's you and I'm sorry

that I haven't left anything here for you in a while, but I just had to figure some things out, and one of those things is that I know that no matter what, I want us to be friends. Can you meet me here after school on Wednesday? I have something I want to give you. Something that I have a feeling will find its way to a certain wall.

From,
Your Friend

A haiku tried to write itself that night in Leland Labyrinth, and I didn't know how to finish it or if I could even make it work. But now I know how, because it's not a haiku. It's something else. And it's still me and the words still wander around the page like a curling path and it's filled with drawing and doodles. But you can't really label it because it's just its own thing.

I want to say thank you. I need to say thank you. Without my secret friend, I don't know if I would have figured out that I want to be visible again.

Drawing Conclusions

I do not know the way
to act like something that I'm not
(this haiku's off two beats now
—it's much harder than I thought)
so maybe this something else that swirls and
    curls and dives
and doesn't stay and wait all day
(or have a perfect rhyme)
and doesn't stay inside the maze
(a perfect one or not)
and doesn't do the things that other people
    think it ought
I think it might be something else that's
    coming from my heart
and if I dare to write in air please know it's
    just my art.
Conclusions drawn by someone else
might leave me all alone
but here's a secret I have found...

Here, I drew a tiny door in a hedge that opens to reveal the last line:

I can draw my own.

I roll the poem up. It's too big to fit into the Portal, but the thing is, I want to hand it to my secret-not-so-secret friend myself.

In person.

Because it's important to say thank you.

Chapter 58

On Wednesday after school, I am waiting by the Wall.

It's funny how much time I've spent here waiting for someone to arrive and let me know that everything is going to be okay or everything is going to work out, and it makes me wonder if there really is ever any one person who can do all that for you.

And then, just like that.

Just like all year.

There is the rustle of leaves and the snapping of twigs. Only, this time, I am smiling as I wait for a flash of color to appear around the bend, because there's nothing better than when the person you've been waiting for finally arrives.

Chapter 59

etunia?" I grab him so he can't run away. "Are you lost? Where is—"

Then Sammie is standing there.

"Hi," she says. She kneels down and scratches him behind the ears. "Isn't he a smart boy?" She smiles. "I've been training him to come find me after school."

I don't know what to say because I don't have time to figure Sammie out right now. We talked at the labyrinth. And then we didn't talk when we got back to school. I just need her to leave before Briggs comes. I don't want a witness when I have to tell the nicest boy I've ever met that I like him so much, but I don't know if I like him the way I heard he likes me, but is it okay if we just keep hanging out and being friends and—oh, by the way, here's a poem I wrote for your wall.

"I really can't talk right now," I say. I crane my neck and try to look behind her.

"Oh," she says. "But I thought—"

"I'm waiting for someone." I don't mean to sound rude, but I need her to leave. Now.

Sammie looks at me. "I know. You're—you're waiting for me."

"What do you mean?" I really need this conversation to end.

Wait.

What *does* she mean?

"You asked me to come," she says. "Wednesday after school. Didn't you—didn't you know it was me? In your note you said you *knew* it was me. You said you had something for me. Something for the Wall." She motions toward the Portal.

It doesn't make sense. How can Sammie be—how can she possibly be the one who—

"But—but how did—how did you even know to—"

Sammie bites her lip. "When you ran out of class the day Dan did that maze presentation, I kind of—I ran after you."

What?

"You did?"

"Yeah. I even got in trouble. I had to listen to this whole lecture from Mr. Clarke about how all it takes is one person, and then another, and the next thing you know the whole class is running out."

I am trying to piece this together, because Sammie is saying things that a few months ago I would have done anything to hear. But now they just confuse me.

"But when I got here, I hid. Because...we hadn't talked in so long and my mom wanted me to drive in with Allegra and her dad every day and his car only has room for him and—well, the four of us, so I couldn't ask you to come, and I just didn't know what to do or say and then—then I saw you with the invisible ink and stuff. Just like the—the secret club book we had and I knew it was for me. It was...wasn't it?"

I nod.

Sammie throws her arms around me. "I knew

it!" She squeezes me. "This year has been the worst. I mean, Allegra—she can be kind of bossy, and I just missed you, but I didn't know if you were mad and—I just didn't know what to do. I mean, we're supposed to do this together and we had all these plans and it hasn't been the same—"

I'm still standing there stiffly. She lets go.

"What? What's wrong?"

"Why didn't you say something sooner?" I ask.

Sammie twists her hands together. "I told you. It's—it's complicated. I didn't know how and—and you didn't exactly say anything to me, either."

"How complicated is it to talk to your best friend just once in—in ten weeks? And I did say something—I said something to you at the pool party. I stood in your living room, dripping wet—in front of Allegra—and you didn't say a word! Do you know how that made me feel?"

"Well—well, what about the way you make *me* feel? Like, I'm so sorry I don't want to dance like a crazy person in the street—and I don't listen to the right radio station—and I don't like the same books you do—it doesn't mean you have to make me feel bad!"

I open my mouth and close it. I didn't know I had made Sammie feel bad. About any of those things. "I'm—I'm sorry. Why didn't you *say* something?"

Her face crumples. "I don't even care about that. I don't want to fight. I miss you. I want us to be... you and me, again."

You and me. My eyes begin to sting. Because this is Sammie. My best friend for my whole life. My Person. What if you *could* start over when things don't go the way you planned? What if you could go back?

"... It's not the same without you," she says.

I nod. "For me, either."

"And I—I asked Allegra if you could hang out with us."

I don't respond for a second. "You *asked*?"

Sammie nods. "Yes! And she said it was okay and that she didn't really mind you anymore. Especially lately, because you haven't been so—well, you know..."

I just look at her.

"You know what I mean...." Sammie says.

I think I do.

I think I know exactly what she means: lately, I haven't been so...

Painting.

Dancing.

Singing.

Laughing.

Open...Feeling...Diving...

"Me," I say. "Lately, I haven't been so *me.*"

Sammie doesn't answer right away. "Why do you sound—all I'm saying is if you could just—"

At that moment, Will and Jaime come crashing through the path with Briggs behind them.

Jaime is saying, "It's a vintage Casio keyboard, Will. You don't have to be a professional musician. Anyone can play it—and that's not what the band's about. It's about having fun—"

Will sees me and stops. "You said you'd be at the middle exit five minutes after the last bell every day, and I told you that I didn't want to, but I still went and waited, and you weren't there. You can't wait for some-one who isn't going to be there for you."

I blink. "What did you say?"

Will sighs. "I repeat: you can't wait for someone who isn't going to be there—"

"No, no, I know *that*." I look at him. "I mean—you waited for me? Will, you hate waiting."

Will pauses. "I can wait."

My face is doing that thing again. That thing that means I'm smiling way too hard. Or maybe I'm smiling exactly the right amount. I don't know. I don't think it matters.

"Hey, Sammie!" says Briggs. "Hey, Petunia—good boy! This is Jaime."

Sammie looks at Jaime and nods.

"Hi," Jaime says. She glances at me, then begins to reach for her headphones. "Um, I guess...maybe I'll just see you guys later."

She's going? Briggs should say something. He's the one who thinks it's important to always say stuff. That things can't get better until—

"Jaime!"

Wait. Who said—

She turns and looks at me.

Oh.

"I..." I look at Briggs and he nods at me. "I...have some ideas for the band...like epic songs, I mean."

"Really?" Jaime smiles just the littlest bit. "You do?"

"Yes, and if...if you want to hang out, I kind of want you to meet my dad."

"Oh. Well, that'd be...um, nice."

Ugh. "No, I mean because my dad is—he wrote *Life of Sky*. He's a—"

"GET OUT!" she shouts. "*Your dad is Steve Lee?*" She turns to Briggs. "Did you know this? Why didn't you tell me?"

Briggs shrugs. "Guess I was more like *Get out! His daughter is Beatrix Lee?*"

I laugh and smile at Briggs. He smiles back.

"Anyway," he says, "Will thinks we should walk the path together from now on. You know, before and after school." He grins. "Jaime just followed along because she's jealous that she doesn't live on a path street—ow!" He laughs and jumps to the side as Jaime swats at him.

"If I ride my bike to your house in the morning, I can walk with you guys," she says. She points far right. "Where does this one go?"

I glance over. "It connects to...everything. You can go anywhere."

"Cool," she says. "We should explore. Do you guys want to explore?"

Briggs looks at me with his full-wattage Briggs smile. "Do you want to? See what's there?" And I'm nodding even though Briggs and I both know that anyone who grew up near these paths knows them inside out already. Kind of in the same way we both know that every path is as new as the day you walk it. "Coming too, Sammie?" he asks.

Sammie.

Sammie is still here. Just watching and not saying a word. I turn to her. But I don't know what to say, either. We stare at each other for a long minute.

Then she shakes her head.

And turns and walks away.

And there's nothing to do but stand there and watch her go. Down the path. And away from me and the clearing and our Wall and all the things that made us an Us for as long as I can remember.

"Is she okay?" asks Briggs. "Should we wait?"

I shake my head no even as my eyes begin to blur. I take a step toward the others. And my foot hits something.

A small bottle. Filled with lemon juice and three drops of water.

I kneel down and pick it up.

And look at it a long time.

You can read about a lot of different things in books. Stories about people in difficult situations. Cartoons about how to make invisible ink and how long it takes for someone to come with a light. But the thing is, after the books are done, you can start to figure things out for yourself. Things that might be similar. Or completely different. And I think what I've figured out right now is that no matter what situation you're in, there is a kind of light you will always have with you—and you don't have to wait for anyone to bring it.

But sometimes it helps.

I stand back up.

"Go ahead," I say, and I turn and run down the path after Sammie, my feet pounding into the ground. "Sammie!" I call out. "Wait!"

Up ahead, she stops and turns. When she sees I'm alone, she rushes toward me, but Petunia gets there first, howling and jumping around my feet, nipping at my jeans.

"You came!" she says. "I knew you'd—what is it?"

It takes me a minute to answer because I'm out of breath.

"I just wanted to let you know that...if you ever wanted...we..." I wave back toward Will, Briggs, and Jaime, and she goes very still. "We're going to meet at the Wall in the mornings to walk to school together."

She doesn't say anything.

I hold out the rolled-up paper. "This...is for you."

She still hasn't moved or said a word, so I put the poem in her hand and wait till her fingers close around it before I let go and then turn and walk away. And I don't know what will happen next, and maybe another person would not have gone back and reached out, but I don't care. I'm the only one who gets to walk my path, and I'm the only one who gets to choose which way to go, and this is the only way I know how to *be*—and I can't leave someone feeling like they're in a dead end without letting them know that there might be a way through.

When I get back to the clearing by the Wall, I stop and turn in a slow full circle, breathing in the air of this place where so much has happened while I've sat waiting. I listen and there's not a footstep or the snap of a twig or the rustling of leaves. I'm alone, but it doesn't feel like it did before and I think that, maybe, it's because the person I was waiting for finally showed up.

"I'm here!" I call out as I run after Will and Briggs and Jaime.

When I turn the corner, Jaime smiles and points to her headphones. "Bea, *c'mon*!" she yells. "Something epic's about to start!"

I hurry over, laughing and nodding and pulling my headphones on, and as she clicks me in, the song playing is so loud and happy and silly, it fills every molecule in my head and my body and my brain and then it fills the whole woods and world and sky and it's like we can't help it—we start running faster and faster and faster, and maybe Briggs and Will can keep up and maybe they can't, but either way is okay, because now we're dancing and laughing and tearing down the path till it feels like flying, and I know—I know if I closed my eyes for just a second, I'd see every color of the rainbow streaming out behind me.

Songs

"Changes"—David Bowie (the Strange Train song)

"Let's Go Crazy"—Prince (pool diving in Taiwan song)

"Free to Be You and Me"—the New Seekers (bath bomb dive song)

"Nobody's Fool"—Avril Lavigne (cousins' girl-power song)

"Groove Is in the Heart"—Deee-Lite (Jaime's *Horton Hears a Who* song)

"Brick House"—the Commodores (S's mom's dance song)

"Ballroom Blitz"—Tia Carrere (S's mom's jump-up-and-down song)

"Unwritten"—Natasha Bedingfield (S's mom's theme song)

"The Middle"—Jimmy Eat World (Bea's things-will-get-better song)

"Control"—Janet Jackson (Jaime's trolls-having-breakfast song)

"Where Does the Good Go?"—Tegan and Sara (TV doctors' last dance-it-out song)

"Candy Girl"—New Edition (candy store montage song)

"The Way I Am"—Ingrid Michaelson (Bea's parents' slow dance/family dance song)

"O-o-h Child"—the Five Stairsteps (car-to-the-hospital song)

"Brave"—Sara Bareilles (Bea listens)

"Hold On Tight"—Electric Light Orchestra (running-down-the-path-with-Jaime song)

Acknowledgments

When you write about a character who has lost her friend group, you become more aware than ever of the people you choose to surround yourself with. Bea's love of poetry, her artistry, her connection to music all came to life for me through the kind of inspiration I was lucky enough to find on a daily basis because of these people. I am and will always be grateful for the wonderful children's book publishing community.

Warmest thanks go to my agent, Sarah Davies of Greenhouse Literary.

To my team at Little, Brown Books for Young Readers: Alvina Ling, Lisa Yoskowitz, Allison Moore, Hallie Tibbetts, Marcie Lawrence, Victoria Stapleton, Jenny Choy, Marisa Finkelstein, Barbara Perris, Sherri Schmidt, Ashley Mason, and everyone else who worked on this book.

To the Society of Children's Book Writers and Illustrators for the support and inspiration. Writers! Join SCBWI!

Bea could never have found her way onto the page

without the help of the many friends who provided information, introductions, or just safe deadline-writing space along the way, especially the keepers and tenders of the Cold Spring Harbor Library, WOMG, and Kidlit Authors of Color. Thanks to my dear Quadrangle (Joyce Wan, Marcie Colleen, and Amber Alvarez), Lynda Mullaly Hunt, Margo Rowder, and Konstantine Anthony. Writing a character with Asperger's was eye-opening. Amid all my research, Rebecca Burgess's insightful comic "Understanding the Spectrum" (theoraah.tumblr .com/post/142300214156/understanding-the-spectrum) truly stood out to me. Her illustration of the autistic spectrum as a multifaceted, color-filled wheel, as opposed to the simple linear image most people think of, beautifully illustrates how different each individual is—along with how alike this makes all of us. This experience has made me even more determined to always continue learning and growing as a writer and working toward sensitivity and understanding of all the complex and wonderful humans we share this planet with.

And speaking of complex and wonderful humans, love and thanks to my family, Peter, Jaz, and Tiger. The loves of my life.